"Kidnapped?" Alejandro barely glanced up from his cell phone when Sienna confronted him in the dining room. "Don't you think that's overly dramatic?"

His gaze pierced her then. Okay, guilty as charged, but she was going to become a mother, and that required strength and resolve. "What would you call leaving London without informing the only remaining guest on board that the Acosta Dragon was sailing?"

"Hospitality?"

She wasn't fooled by Alejandro's relaxed manner. That wasn't a joke. Tension radiated from him in suffocating waves. "Just tell me why you've done this, Alejandro."

"I would have thought that was obvious." Lifting his head, he studied her without warmth. "Why did you hide the fact that you're pregnant?"

"I didn't hide it—"

"You just didn't get around to telling me?"

The chilling timbre of his voice made it sound as if they were two strangers who had never shared a moment's intimacy, and all that had ever been between them was sex.

"I only just found out myself."

Welcome to the world of

The Acostas!

Passion, temptation and seduction!

Meet Argentina's most scandalous family!
Follow these notorious heartbreakers' legacies
in these other sizzling stories by *USA TODAY*
bestselling author Susan Stephens:

The Untamed Argentinian
The Shameless Life of Ruiz Acosta
The Argentinian's Solace
A Taste of the Untamed
The Man From Her Wayward Past
Taming the Last Acosta
Christmas Nights with the Polo Player
One Scandalous Christmas Eve
The Playboy Prince of Scandal
Forbidden to Her Spanish Boss
Kidnapped for the Acosta Heir

All available now!

Susan Stephens

KIDNAPPED FOR THE ACOSTA HEIR

HARLEQUIN
PRESENTS

HARLEQUIN®
PRESENTS™

Recycling programs
for this product may
not exist in your area.

ISBN-13: 978-1-335-58443-4

Kidnapped for the Acosta Heir

Copyright © 2023 by Susan Stephens

For questions and comments about the quality of this book, please contact us at CustomerService@Harlequin.com.

Harlequin Enterprises ULC
22 Adelaide St. West, 41st Floor
Toronto, Ontario M5H 4E3, Canada
www.Harlequin.com

Printed in U.S.A.

Susan Stephens was a professional singer before meeting her husband on the Mediterranean island of Malta. In true Harlequin style, they met on Monday, became engaged on Friday and married three months later. Susan enjoys entertaining, travel and going to the theater. To relax, she reads, cooks and plays the piano, and when she's had enough of relaxing, she throws herself off mountains on skis or gallops through the countryside singing loudly.

Books by Susan Stephens

Harlequin Presents

Snowbound with His Forbidden Innocent

Passion in Paradise

A Scandalous Midnight in Madrid
A Bride Fit for a Prince?

Secret Heirs of Billionaires

The Secret Kept from the Greek

The Acostas!

One Scandalous Christmas Eve
The Playboy Prince of Scandal
Forbidden to Her Spanish Boss

Visit the Author Profile page
at Harlequin.com for more titles.

Huge thanks to you, my loyal readers, for loving my Acosta guys. I thought there would be five Acosta stories, but with your encouragement, those sizzling-hot bad boys just kept leaping onto the page!

Thanks to my family for their good humor and patience, and my friends for the same. Not forgetting my scrupulous and effective editor, Nic, and every member of the team it takes to make a book. And of course, my husband for his unstinting love and support.

Happy reading everyone!

CHAPTER ONE

HE BURNED LIKE a fire in the centre of the room. Outwardly cool and contained, and good-looking beyond the bounds of reason, Alejandro Acosta was rugged and tanned like a man who spent less time behind a desk than he did riding horses on the vast landholding he ruled over in Spain.

And his eyes. *Dark eyes that seemed to plumb her soul.*

What did she know about him? Apart from the fact that he had been her late brother Tom's best friend and was a member of the immensely powerful Acosta family, Sienna knew precisely nothing.

His glance washed over her with indifference. 'Won't you sit down?'

Acosta's voice was deeply masculine, and almost insultingly brusque. She'd heard it said that Alejandro had continued to work for the army long after he left the forces. Tom had let slip that having made a fortune in tech, prior to his service in the regiment, Alejandro had recently been tasked with trialling a special type of drone on the battlefield. Tom had explained that Alejandro was one of many subcontractors, drafted in to fulfil a specific task for the military. It must have been this that had brought them together on that fateful night. With his first-hand knowledge of the army's requirements, and one of Alejandro's companies being a world leader in the field of drone surveillance, he was the perfect man for the job.

But not the perfect man to be standing to attention alongside, Sienna seethed as he continued to try and stare her down. 'I'm happy standing, thank you.'

The disapproving lift of one sweeping ebony brow was his answer to that.

He didn't trouble to hide the fact that he found the presence of a stranger in his London home distasteful. Hostile vibes pinged off him in waves. Sienna wasn't exactly thrilled to be revisiting her grief at the loss of her brother in front of such a cold man. It was only a matter of weeks since Tom had been killed, and his funeral was still a raw memory. She'd rather be anywhere than here in Alejandro Acosta's plush study, being confronted by an ice king, and a cold-faced solicitor, for the reading of her brother's will. She'd rushed here half dressed for the club where she sang each night, because this was the only time that suited Señor Acosta, his PA had informed Sienna. The fact that the timing couldn't have been worse for Sienna didn't seem to register. Acosta issued orders, and everyone snapped to attention, she presumed.

The most enigmatic of the Spanish Acosta brothers, Alejandro Acosta was so powerful, so rich, he was untouchable, and had made himself unreachable to all except the privileged few. For the short time she was here, Sienna was briefly one of that small number.

'Sit.'

She jerked to attention at the sound of his voice, and immediately wished she hadn't. What a rude man. Fortunately, their paths were unlikely to cross again, as they inhabited two very different worlds. Sienna's was hand to mouth, but full of drive and optimism, or it had been until Tom's death, while, according to the press, Alejandro's financial worth was incalculable, but his wealth didn't seem to have made him happy.

A glance at her watch told her what she already knew. She was going to be late at the Blue Angel, where she was the headline act. The club was on the other side of London, and the manager was strict about timekeeping. Sienna was too. She cared deeply about her audience, and couldn't bear to think about them being disappointed, simply because Alejandro Acosta cared for nothing and no one but himself. And there were practical concerns. If she lost her job at the club, how would she pay her final college fees? The bursar had been understanding up to now, in allowing Sienna to spread the cost of her course, but without that precious certificate to prove she was a qualified music therapist, years of study would be wasted.

As the seconds ticked away Sienna's panic mounted. Respectable singing jobs were hard to find. The last place she'd attended for an audition had told her that entertainers were only hired to keep their punters happy. It hadn't seemed important if she could sing or not, and although the Blue Angel wasn't the type of sophisticated venue she imagined Acosta frequenting, neither was it a seedy cover for anything else. People came to the club to eat good food, and listen to great music, not to hit on the staff.

The glance at her wristwatch had drawn Acosta's attention. Lifting her chin, she stared back. She had never encountered a man so aloof and cold, who could, she admitted now, be so dangerously sensual too. The very model of a billionaire, he had dressed for the occasion in an impeccably tailored dark suit. Black diamonds flashed at the cuffs of his pristine white shirt, in a reminder, had she needed one, that the man's tailoring alone had probably cost more than she earned in a month. Another anxious glance at the door drew his scathing look.

'Are we keeping you, Ms Slater?'

His voice was a low, husky baritone, betraying barely the hint of an accent. 'Sienna, please,' she said politely. They could at least make the pretence of being civil to each other in front of the solicitor. 'I explained to your PA that this is the worst possible time for me.'

'I'm sure you'll *make* time to hear the detail of your brother's substantial bequest in your favour. Oh, and please,' he added with a sarcastic edge, 'call me Alejandro.'

She could think of something else to call him. The expression on his face was distinctly mocking. No wonder, she conceded, when she had dashed here, half dressed for the club, looking like a party girl, fun interrupted on a Friday night, calling in to hear what her brother, barely cold in his grave, had left her.

The cool grey gaze of the lawyer, seated in Alejandro's place behind his desk, added to her discomfort as he levelled a silent reprimand on her face. 'Please carry on,' she said in an attempt to ignore Alejandro's lowering presence.

This request was directed to the solicitor, but as his droning delivery started up again she was uncomfortably aware of Alejandro's primal heat and clean man scent as it filled her senses. Turning her thoughts determinedly to Tom, the brother she'd adored, Sienna could only marvel at how different Tom had been from Alejandro, his so-called best friend. Her brother's appetite for life had been insatiable. Full of kindness and laughter, Tom had had a wicked sense of humour that could always make her smile—

'Something amusing you, Ms Slater?'

Alejandro's question put her on edge. Her only crime was smiling as she thought about Tom. 'I was thinking about my brother, and how much I loved him. And how Tom could always make me laugh.' She might have been diminished by grief, but she hadn't been destroyed by it, and neither Alejandro nor the solicitor could find a clever answer to that.

Hearing the contents of Tom's will left Sienna stunned. She'd had no idea that her brother had accumulated so much money, or that he would leave it all to Sienna. Since the day their parents were tragically killed in a car crash, when she was fourteen, and Tom just four years older, Tom had promised to look after her, but this was on another level. All she wanted was some small memento from Tom, and an expression of love. Her troubled gaze landed on an army photograph, standing square on Alejandro's desk. Alejandro spearheaded the squad of good-looking men, but Tom stood out with his easy smile, and boy-next-door good looks. Once again she asked herself: how could Tom buddy up with this cold man?

Looking back, she'd been muddled by grief and shock when the officers from Tom's regiment had told her the terrible news. They'd said something about Alejandro being involved... Her questioning glance clashed with his. She held his stare steadily. Why, oh, why hadn't Tom saved himself first?

Trouble. That was the first thing that came to mind when he assessed Tom's sister, Sienna. A pale scrap of a woman with long, fiery red hair, she had dressed as if she intended to party hard on the news that Tom had left her a great deal of money, together with Tom's substantial landholding on an island off the coast of Spain—an island Alejandro owned half of. He had successfully avoided feeling anything for years, but Tom's death had opened old wounds that threatened his control in front of this woman.

Returning his attention to the solicitor, who had just asked them both to please sit for the reading of a letter from Tom, he informed the man, 'I'll remain standing.'

He had to hide his shock as the solicitor read on. The contents of Tom's will had been bad enough, and, in fairness, Tom's sister appeared equally perplexed as she listened to the contents of the letter.

Alejandro, I'd trust you with my life, but don't mess with my sister.

Was he to take that as a challenge from the grave? It was followed by some mush for Sienna, along the lines of: I'll always love you, and all I ask is that you follow your dreams.

There were tears in Sienna's eyes. She needn't worry. Tom could have spared himself the trouble of writing those words. Snagged black stockings, a too tight skirt, teamed with a garish, sequined top, brought only one thought to Alejandro's mind: 'Not a chance.' In fact, he found it incredible that, thanks to the terms of Tom's will, he now owned the island he loved jointly with this woman. And there was more to it than that. Tom had got lucky on the stock market, and had wanted to do something useful with the money. They'd come up with the idea of building a rehabilitation centre for veterans on the island. Alejandro had been delighted that Tom had seized upon this idea, as he'd hoped they'd found something at last to save Tom.

That project would still happen, he silently pledged. Nothing and no one would stand in his way. A living testament to Tom would still be built.

And Sienna? What would she have to say about it?

Life was full of challenges. She was just one more.

As if reading his thoughts, she glanced up. Challenge flared in her eyes. He was instantly suspicious. What was she up to? His body didn't care, and responded with enthusiasm to the defiance in her steady gaze. Naturally, his mind overruled his body. She simply wasn't his type. Tom had described his sister as zany and fun, though she could be stubborn, Tom had excused. From what Alejandro had seen, Sienna Slater was unpredictable and bold, which could be a problem. When he'd asked Tom where she worked, Tom had been evasive. 'She works in a club,' Tom had said. 'Tells me she has a really big secret to share with me very soon.' Tom had laughed rather awkwardly as he'd said this, adding, 'I hope she hasn't got herself pregnant.' There hadn't been much Alejandro could say to that.

Returning his thoughts to the island he and Tom's sister now shared, he realised the solution was simple. He'd buy her out. Tom would applaud his decision. It would ensure that Sienna had everything she could possibly need going forward into whatever murky style of life she chose. Tom's last words on the battlefield, his last thoughts, had been for Sienna.

'Tell Sienna I love her, and always will, wherever this new adventure takes me.'

Alejandro had heard it said that people could find no fault in those they loved in their last moments. That had certainly been true in Tom's case. In respect for his friend, Alejandro would do everything in his power to make sure that Sienna was safe, and wanted for nothing—

His chin jerked up. 'You're leaving?' he asked with surprise as she made for the door.

The solicitor was also packing up, he noticed now.

'These documents are for both of you—a copy each,' the lawyer said on his way out of the door. 'Mull them over at your leisure.'

'Thank you...'

Sienna's soft tone captured Alejandro's attention, and he was forced to admit that he'd never seen anyone look quite so sad before. In that moment, he was glad she hadn't seen her brother's broken body, or been forced to endure the terrible silence when he'd gone. He wouldn't tell her. It would break anyone's heart.

It wasn't his job to mend hearts, but it was his responsibility to keep a watching brief on Sienna.

'"Until my sister feels comfortable with her new situation, I'm entrusting my friend Alejandro with the management of Sienna's inheritance..."'

The solicitor had sighed with disapproval as

he'd read this out, but it did mean that Alejandro had the final say when it came to any plans Sienna might have for the island, as well as how she used her newly inherited wealth. The lawyer had gone on to explain that he'd dealt with many similar wills where the deceased had unintentionally, if with the best of intentions, made things difficult for those left behind.

The wall clock behind him began to chime, which was Sienna's cue to exclaim with concern, 'I'm late.'

He bridled. What could possibly be more important to this woman, than the reading of her brother's will?

'I'm singing tonight,' she explained to the room at large.

With an angry gesture, he exclaimed, 'For goodness' sake, go!' Bad enough he should be forced to expose his feelings for Tom, without Tom's sister insinuating that he was keeping her here under duress. Tom wasn't supposed to die. Tom's sister wasn't supposed to inherit half the island. The fact that he, Alejandro, the most meticulous of men, had overlooked the possibility that such a disaster could occur only made his growing tension blaze higher.

But then he saw her face.

Riven with shock, she looked broken. What was wrong with him? They had both lost a piece of their life. Sienna had lost a brother. He only had to think back to how broken his siblings had been when their parents were killed to know how long grief took to heal.

'Before I go…' There was no challenge in her voice now.

'Yes?'

'I know how close you were to Tom.' She said this staring straight into his eyes. 'I want to thank you for everything you did for him.'

'Thank me?' He drew back. 'Thank me for what?'

'For taking my place with Tom at the end,' she explained.

What did she know about *the end*? What could anyone know? Sienna would have been informed in the broadest terms about Tom's injuries, but did she know that the real battle had been in her brother's mind? It wasn't up to him to tell her. How would it benefit Sienna to know?

He made a dismissive gesture in an attempt to close the subject. 'You don't have to thank me for anything.' The island he'd shared with Tom had been intended to restore her brother to the man Sienna thought she knew. It was a blessing she'd never seen how the weight of battle had crushed Tom, who was not just a brave soldier before his mind crashed, but a man who always went above and beyond for his comrades. Alejandro would remember Tom as a hero, a man who battled demons both real and imagined, and who was like a true brother to him. He would always be in Tom's debt.

'I'll say goodbye, then…'

He turned to see Sienna standing at the door. What did she want from him? 'You do realise Tom's money won't come through immediately?'

'I know that.'

She flinched as if he'd hit her, and her voice sounded raw, but he pushed on. 'I'm happy to extend a loan, for however long you might need one…'

She frowned and looked perplexed. 'A loan for what?'

He gave a casual shrug. 'For whatever you might need.'

'I don't need anything, thank you.'

He was still suspicious. What did he know about her? Would Sienna be able to resist the lure of his wealth? 'Think about my offer, and come back to me if you need help.'

'I don't need to think about your offer,' she assured him. 'I can't think straight about anything right now, let alone money, but one thing I am sure about is that I don't need your help.'

'Don't be too hasty,' he advised. 'You'll soon have responsibilities—'

'Which I'll handle when I have to,' she interrupted. 'Believe me, I won't be rushing into any hasty decisions.'

A strength had come into her face he hadn't seen before. 'I'm trying to make things easy for you,' he explained.

The cynical lift of one finely drawn brow was accompanied by a cryptic question: 'Are you judging me on appearance, and thinking me needy?'

'No.' Yes, he was. 'Do you intend to hitch a lift to Spain—to visit your land?'

Her answer was a huff of incredulity. 'You have no idea of my means, and although I'm *very grateful* for your offer, please don't trouble yourself to make another, as I can't envisage any situation where I'd seek help from you.'

'We all need something, *señorita*,' he observed, resting back against the wall. 'And you may change your mind. Call me if that happens.' Reaching into the breast pocket of his jacket, he pulled out a card.

Taking the card without looking at it, she moved past him to the door. He opened it for her, and as they brushed against each other her cheeks pinked up. His reaction was more primitive. 'One last word of advice,' he offered through gritted teeth. 'Don't discuss your windfall widely.'

'My *windfall*?' she challenged, swinging

around. 'Are you suggesting I regard my brother's bequest as nothing more than a tax-free win?'

'I *suggest* that you are wilfully misunderstanding me.'

'Am I?' she added with bite.

If looks could kill, but, *Dios*, she was beautiful. Younger than he'd imagined. *Had Tom said twenty-four?* If so, she was a very young twenty-four. Innocence blazed as fiercely as the anger in her eyes. 'I understand that you're upset—' She huffed at this, but, keeping his voice level, he continued, 'I intend no offence, and my offer remains open without time limit—' Was she even listening now? 'Don't forget to take your copy of Tom's letter with you—'

He fully expected her to snatch it from him, and stuff it in the envelope containing her brother's will, but instead she gripped it tightly, as if the paper it was written on contained some remnant of Tom. Her hands were shaking, he noticed, and she seemed emotionally deflated. Even he found it hard not to feel something when tears began to fall unchecked down her face. Examining Sienna's stricken eyes, he knew with certainty that he would never tell her the entire truth about Tom's death.

Reaching past her, he opened the door, but, perhaps remembering the last time when they'd touched, she lifted her hands up as if to ward him off, and her tone was very different as she said, 'I'll be sure to dress appropriately the next time we meet—'

What did he expect her to wear, sackcloth and ashes? But, bizarrely, the notion of a *next* time appealed to him.

'Tell me one thing, Alejandro,' she said, surprising him by stopping dead on her way out of the door.

The passion in her eyes transfixed him. 'Yes?'

'How could a man like you be my brother's best friend?'

He didn't take offence, because he'd asked himself that same question many times. Tom had released something in him, he supposed, until darkness had finally descended on Tom, and there was no lightness left in him.

'Tom was wonderfully warm and funny,' Sienna continued, unaware of the terrible irony in her words. 'My brother was the kindest person I ever knew. He lived in the light—lived *for* the light. He didn't dwell in darkness like you!'

'Upsetting yourself won't bring Tom back,' he cautioned. His concern was growing that Sienna might actually blunder into the road in this state and do herself some damage.

'Don't tell me to calm down,' she snapped. 'I'm grieving, heartbroken—stressed out with all the information you and the lawyer expect me to digest in an instant—'

'You're obviously distressed—'

'No!' she flared, brushing his hand from her shoulder. 'Don't you dare touch me! How do you think I feel in your gloomy house, with these heavy curtains and blinds shutting out the world? And—' She seemed at a loss for a moment, before blurting, 'And your butler wears white gloves.'

Hysteria born out of grief, he supposed, deciding to treat it with gentle humour. 'You take exception to white gloves?'

'I take exception to this hideous house,' she retorted.

His London residence had been decked out by an award-winning interior designer, who, she had told him, had taken great pains to reflect his personality. Unfortunately, he could see now that Sienna had a point, saying it was gloomy.

'And this!' she continued, jolting him back into the moment. Sweeping aside the curtains, she allowed the acid light of street lamps to flood into the room. 'I take exception to you! If you allowed some light into your life, perhaps you'd see things more clearly.' And with that, she stormed into the hall.

'Thank you, I'll see myself out,' he heard her declare, and then the front door closed behind her, leaving heavy silence in Sienna's wake.

CHAPTER TWO

IT TOOK SIENNA a good few minutes after leaving Alejandro's house to realise that she must be in shock. Meeting someone she had imagined would be like Tom, only to find Alejandro so very different, had rattled her to the point where grief for Tom threatened to overwhelm her.

She'd always found it easy to express herself through song, and couldn't get to Soho fast enough. How she got there was another mystery. She was on autopilot, with her thoughts reeling as her feet found the way.

Tom's bequest had left her speechless. She'd had no idea he had so much money. And half an island? Incredible. But why hadn't he said something the last time they'd been together? They'd spoken on the phone, she remembered, thinking back. Tom had given no hint of impending danger. How could he, when the nature of his job meant that everything had to be kept top secret? He'd been upbeat as usual, and had

quickly turned the focus on Sienna. As usual.
She should have pressed him for more details
about his life—

Would the guilt ever stop?

This was all such a mess. The meeting with
Alejandro had only made things worse, by going
as badly as it could. She didn't like the man and
could tell he didn't like her. There was nothing
to be done about it. Convincing Alejandro that
she had never wanted anything from Tom, except his love, was a lost cause. All she wanted
was her brother back.

Why had Tom made it a condition of his
will that she had to ask Alejandro for permission each time she wanted to use the money in
Tom's bequest? Didn't he trust her? Nothing
in their past pointed to that. If the idea hadn't
been so preposterous, she might imagine Tom
had thrown them together on purpose.

That thought was enough to make her shiver
with awareness and dread. Alejandro was like
two sides of the same coin. One side rubbed her
up the wrong way, while the other held a fatal
fascination. She couldn't think of a better reason to keep her distance from him.

Thoughts splintering into a thousand different
strands, she dipped her head to barrel through
the biting London wind. After the sedate pace
of Mayfair, hurrying to the club through such

a lively, bustling area was almost a relief. The contrast with Alejandro in his sombre Georgian mansion, located in a silent upmarket street, made her smile. She lived in a bedsit in someone else's house, in a not very fashionable part of London, but at least her room was bright and cheery, and she'd been happy living there, until Tom's death, while Alejandro didn't look the least bit happy.

Catching sight of the club always lifted Sienna's spirits. There was the customary long line of eager patrons, snaking around the building, waiting for the doors to open. Music had always saved her. When she'd lost her parents, she'd turned to music as a way to express her grief. Looking for a way to support herself, she turned to music again. And when Tom died, she found solace in singing.

An appreciative audience was a gift beyond price. They didn't come to the Blue Angel to see long faces. It was an opportunity to leave their troubles behind for an hour or two, and she was happy to join them in that. Losing Tom had been like a light going out of Sienna's life, but during the reading of the will she had realised that Tom had lit the light of possibility. And no one, not even the formidable Alejandro Acosta, was going to stand in the way of that.

Rex, the doorman, ushered her through the waiting queue. Rex didn't wear white gloves. Rex didn't wear any gloves. His knuckles bore many scars, but he was a kindly man, a widower with a heart of gold, who did everything for his two school-aged children. Patrons of the club only knew him as King Rex, a man they wouldn't dare to cross, but if Rex liked them he might ask Sienna if he could bring them to meet her.

'No visitors backstage tonight, Rex,' she said regretfully. 'I'm going to leave as soon as I finish my last set.'

Rex sympathised immediately, because he understood. 'You must be exhausted. Your brother…' Rex shook his head as he shrugged in sympathy.

'You too,' Sienna said gently. 'I hope you know how much we all appreciate you being here, when your life has been turned upside down?'

'You and my children are the ray of light that keeps me going,' he said, making Sienna wish that a ray of light could penetrate Alejandro's dark world. For a moment there, she felt sorry for him.

The following day, while Alejandro was straightening the picture of Tom on his desk, he thought about Sienna. He'd thought of little else. Unused to wealth, she would be vulnerable to predators. He had to find a way to persuade her to come to him for both money and advice.

Don't mess with my sister. The words rang in

his head. What had Tom meant by that warning? Tom knew full well that Alejandro's taste ran to sophisticated women who knew the score. You needn't worry, he silently informed his old friend. Your sister is safe from me.

If that were true, why was he still thinking about her?

The challenge in Sienna's eyes was to blame, he concluded. Who knew what she had in mind when it came to Tom's money and land? He'd have to see her again in order to set parameters, and, in truth, he'd like to hear her sing. Anything he could learn about Sienna would help him when it came to interpreting her intentions going forward.

Is that the only reason I want to see her again?

What else could it be?

There weren't many things forbidden to Alejandro Acosta, but Tom Slater's sister was one of them.

He dredged his mind for snippets of information that Tom might have told him about Sienna. His main concern was that Tom had always sounded tense when he talked about his sister. In Tom's opinion, Sienna had left school too soon, in order to pursue a career in music. 'She's headstrong,' Tom had explained, 'and refuses to listen to me.'

Hmm. She would have to listen to Alejandro.

Headstrong or not, Sienna wouldn't receive a penny of her inheritance unless she—

Unless she what? Kowtowed to him?

Recalling those fiery green eyes, he knew the road ahead wouldn't be easy, and, strangely, he looked forward to embarking on that journey. Gazing at Tom's photograph again, he had to wonder, how could one sibling become a tortured hero, while the other appeared content to work in a club?

Necessity? his interfering inner critic suggested.

He dismissed this out of hand. Club work was not a safe option for a woman who had recently inherited a fortune in money and land.

Those fiery green eyes should see her through?

Unlikely, he thought as he cleaned the already clean photo frame with his sleeve. The action prompted him to study Tom's face. Tom certainly didn't seem on the surface like a deeply troubled man, which was why the army had deemed him fit for service. He'd shared the island with Tom in the hope that it would give Tom the chance to build a new life away from the battlefield. And now he would build a fitting memorial to the dearest of friends.

The irony of a friendship based on mutual guilt had not escaped him. Neither he nor Tom had ever forgiven themselves for their parents' deaths.

If only we'd done this, or that, we might have stopped them. That had been a common theme between them. And now Sienna found herself in the middle of that turmoil, which made finding the right way to deal with her twice as hard.

Sienna sang her heart out that night at the club, dedicating each song in her mind to Tom. Jason, her accompanist on the piano, sensing her intense involvement in the music, had played like an angel. The audience couldn't have been more responsive or warmer if they'd tried. She would never be able to thank them enough for the distraction they provided.

The surprises in Tom's will hadn't helped to settle her mind. Nor had the fact that Tom had gone, while Alejandro Acosta was very much here, and very much in her life. That said, however powerful he was, she would not be browbeaten, and whether Alejandro agreed or not she would find a way to turn Tom's bequest into a living memorial for everything her brother had stood for.

The club organised a cab to take her home each night, and once she was safely inside her tiny bedsit she ran through the solicitor's words in her mind, but thoughts of Alejandro proved a constant distraction. Leaning back against the thin padding of a threadbare chair, she wondered what Alejandro thought of her. He was a living symbol of success, but that didn't make him compassionate.

Why, Tom, why? I don't want anything from you. I certainly didn't want to meet up with that awful man. I don't want an island, or your money, I just want you back.

But Tom wasn't coming back, and the only way to handle a man like Alejandro Acosta was with endless patience, and as much diplomacy as she could muster.

On that discomforting thought, she switched off the fire and crawled into bed. The covers were so cold they felt damp, and again, thoughts of Alejandro intruded. What an unlikely friend for Tom. There had to be something she didn't know about her brother that had led to his close friendship with Alejandro. If only she hadn't kept news of her recent professional qualification from Tom. She'd paid for her college course by working at the club, but she'd enjoyed that. Turning her face into the pillow, she tried not to be sad. There was so much to be grateful for. Music was her life, and, thanks to Tom's generosity in his will, she could build a centre in his name, and share music with countless others—

Even Alejandro?

She all but growled when his face came into her head, and all chance of sleep was lost. Reaching for the light, she climbed out of bed. Shrugging on her outdoor coat to fend off the chill, she switched on her heater. Ferreting about in her cluttered tote, she found the will and read it again. Would she ever understand Tom's intentions? A vast tract of land *and* all that money? Half an island off the coast of Spain, for someone who, with her studies and work, had rarely travelled out of London. And her land abutted Alejandro's. At first, when the solicitor had read out the will, she'd imagined building a retreat on the island, but later she'd learned that she would have to ask Alejandro's permission to do anything. Well, whatever he thought, she would visit the island and make her own decision about what to do next.

Did that mean meeting up with Alejandro?

Her heart thundered at the thought. Even here, in a tiny room she could cross in five steps, it was as if he occupied every inch of space.

Putting the will away safely, she got back into bed. The frigid covers couldn't compete with the expression she pictured on Alejandro's face, when she pitched her idea for a therapy centre on the island. She resolutely turned her thoughts to sun-kissed beaches instead. It was just a shame that the last image in her mind before the world of sleep claimed her was of a blisteringly handsome man with a jaw set as firm as her own.

CHAPTER THREE

RAGE AT THE injustice of Tom's will soared inside him as he got ready for a night out that Sienna would not expect. What did she know about farming fertile farm land in Spain? What would she do with her portion of the land? Visions of a glitzy shopping mall, or, worse, a forest of high-rise hotels sprang to mind, with Sienna dressed to the nines, fêted on every side by shallow, grasping individuals, all scheming to take advantage of her. The island was easily big enough to warrant development, but that had never been his plan. The islanders didn't want it, and it was up to him to protect them from some badly thought-out scheme.

Rasping a thumbnail across the fast-growing stubble on his face, he glowered into the mirror. Pocketing his phone, he headed out. Turned out, Sienna was the headline act at the Blue Angel tonight. He had to concede that said something about her ability. He'd learned the club was well thought of, and not by those hoping to see and to be seen. The Blue Angel had built its reputation solely on the quality of its musicians, which drove his curiosity where Sienna was concerned.

Beautiful, intriguing and exasperating, he concluded as he gunned the engine of his favourite car. Rebellion glowed in those green, green eyes; emerald eyes with a mix of intelligence and stubbornness blazing from them. By the time he brought his vehicle to a halt outside the club, he had to remind himself firmly that fantasies about emerald eyes were superfluous to requirements.

His arrival had attracted the doorman's attention. That and a fifty. 'I'd like a word with your singer, Sienna Slater,' he explained to the burly bouncer. To his surprise, the man didn't assure him that anything and everything was possible, and instead returned the fifty as he said solemnly, 'If you give me your name, I'll pass your message on.'

Kudos to the man. 'I'd appreciate that, thank you.'

'I'll see your car's parked safely,' the doorman added as he summoned a younger man to take the keys.

'Am I allowed to tip him?' Alejandro asked with some irony.

'As you see fit,' the doorman told him with dignity.

Good man, he thought, acknowledging this with a nod of his head.

He entered the club to find a more than half-decent jazz band playing. He guessed the musicians were warming up the crowd for the main event, which was Sienna. Just that. Just her first name written in gold on a full-sized billboard showing a young woman with wistful green eyes, and a beautiful, if surprisingly mischievous, face. But what really caught his attention was Sienna's spectacular hourglass figure. Far from the defensive waif in shabby clothes he remembered, this was a confident woman with a warm, friendly smile. Tumbling auburn hair completed the picture. Set free to cascade in gleaming waves down her back, the glossy profusion was styled to cover one naked shoulder.

A single word sprang to mind, and it wasn't for public consumption.

The moment she walked on stage Sienna was aware of a brooding presence. Was that really Alejandro standing by the door? *Why was he here?* Heat and shock raced through her. He was staring at her. And only her.

Everyone was staring at her. That tended to happen when you were on stage.

Maybe, she conceded, but only one stare in the club held erotic menace. And, by some alchemy of his own, Alejandro managed to look even more striking than before. Who knew that dressing down could look this sexy? Snug-fitting jeans secured by a heavy-duty belt, with a dark top that clung to his impressive torso with loving attention to detail, was completed by black loafers, black jacket, thick black stubble, and wildly tumbled, wavy black hair.

Did he ever comb that hair, or did he just rake it in frustration each time they met? A steely billionaire was transformed into what looked more like a pirate of old on the loose. Sienna knew which variation she preferred. Her erotic zones did too. But now she had to concentrate, or she'd never be able to sing.

Tearing her gaze away from Alejandro, she almost wished he'd turn back into the cold man at their first meeting. This primal brute, with barely suppressed energy raging off him, was a threat to her senses, and she didn't have enough experience to know how to deal with that. He'd even managed to silence the jokers at the bar, who, after a couple of drinks, thought they could take on the world. Was this dangerous-looking individual the real Alejandro? A shiver coursed down her spine at the thought.

Propping a hip against the wall, he stared

straight back, upping the threat to her senses. Her mouth dried and her throat closed. Would it even be possible to sing? For the first time ever, she missed her musical cue. Thank goodness for Jason at the piano, who took the hitch in his stride, improvising as if his piano solo had been intended all along. Recovering fast, she smiled across at Jason, whose deft touch on the piano reassured Sienna that this was her world, a world where she was comfortable. And this was her music, the same music that had allowed her to pay her way through college with a distinction at the end of her course.

The audience fell quiet as she began to sing. They were attentive throughout and went wild when she finished. Her gaze sought out Alejandro, who nodded his head with approval. She had no idea why his appreciation meant so much to her, just that it did.

Bringing Jason forward to share the applause, she smiled warmly across at her brilliant accompanist, and when the crowd called for more, they were happy to oblige. Once that encore had finished, she refocused to find Alejandro moving towards the stage.

What did he want? Why was he here? She couldn't imagine a club like the Blue Angel would be Señor Acosta's venue of choice. Though tonight, she had to admit, he fitted in

perfectly in casual clothes, though he was causing quite a stir. Several people had recognised
the famous billionaire, polo-playing Acosta
brother from his pictures in the press, and were
transfixed by his striking presence as he walked
through the club.

What was she supposed to do now? She could
hardly invite him into her cupboard-sized dressing room, which she shared with her friend the
boiler and a few crates of beer.

'Alejandro,' she said, as pleasantly as she
could.

'Sienna.'

He made no attempt at all to sound pleasant,
and his shrewd dark eyes pierced her soul with
unforgiving intensity. Ignoring the fact that he
was holding out a hand to help her down the
steps at the side of the stage, she picked up the
hem of her gown and made her own way down.
'I didn't expect to see you here tonight,' she admitted, craning her neck to meet his black stare.
How could she have forgotten how tall he was,
or how big and powerful, and evenly tanned?
At least, she imagined he was evenly tanned...

Stop that! she told herself firmly as the man
in question began to speak. 'I'm sure you didn't
expect to see me here,' he agreed, in the now
familiar dark-chocolate voice.

Be polite. Treat him like a welcome guest.

Don't avoid his stare. Meet it. And smile. 'I hope you enjoyed the show?'

'Very much,' he said, surprising her by sounding as if he meant this.

Alejandro's sexual charge made it hard to keep focus. He made it impossible to look anywhere but into his eyes. Radiating a force that she found almost hypnotic. It was a struggle to blank thoughts of how it might feel to be in his arms.

'I'm sorry,' she said briskly, 'but I need to get changed. My cab will be arriving to take me home soon.'

'There's no need for you to take a cab.'

There was every need to take a cab, she thought, interpreting the smouldering interest in Alejandro's eyes as something it was safer not to get too close to. 'I have to wash off my stage make-up first.'

'Of course,' he allowed.

'If you'll excuse me—?' She tried to move past, but, just as he'd been at the door in his house, Alejandro took up a lot of space. She was intensely aware that the gown she had chosen to wear that evening was a figure-skimming column of silver silk satin that clung to every curve she possessed, the urge to replace it with baggy jeans and an even baggier top was suddenly a priority. Alejandro's expression was calculating, and if she hadn't promised herself to try and keep things smooth with him, she'd tell him straight out that she'd dressed for her audience, not for him.

Sidling past, she opened the door that led down to her basement dressing room, leaving Alejandro and his smouldering look in her wake. Once she was safely enclosed inside the small space, she stared at her reflection in the fly-blown mirror. Her cheeks were flushed. She looked excited, and that was definitely bad news.

Easing out of her gown, she hung it up on a hanger. Reaching for her cleansing cream, she removed every trace of the siren who had sung on the stage. Girl-next-door restored, she felt confidence returning along with her clean, shiny face, and laughed bitterly at the thought that life could not be transformed quite so easily.

But she'd get through this, Sienna determined as she picked up her things. And if she and Alejandro got the chance to know each other a little better, she felt sure he'd see reason when it came to her scheme for a music facility on the island.

Really? You think he'll go for that?

Tom had said a lot of things about Alejandro. One, that he was the bravest man Tom knew, and also the most loyal, as well as being the fairest, so perhaps there was a chance he'd agree to her scheme.

'Alejandro leads from the front, and never leaves a man behind,' Tom had said. This was true, according to the officers who had broken the terrible news to Sienna. Alejandro hadn't left Tom behind. He'd carried Tom's lifeless body through gunfire and explosion, all the way back to camp, where he'd spent that first long night talking to Tom as if he were still alive. On that basis alone, she had to give Alejandro a second chance. She could only trust he'd give her a second chance too.

Firming her resolve, she went upstairs to find Alejandro in the same place, resting back against the wall. 'We need to talk, Sienna. Are you cold?' he asked with concern when she shivered.

Cold? No. Apprehensive? Yes. What was so important it had brought Alejandro to the club tonight? She would not be rushed into any decision when it came to the island.

'Let's go,' he said. 'We can't speak here. It's far too noisy.'

'Go where?' She hung back. 'My cab's due any minute.'

'I've told you before, you don't need a cab. I'll take you home.'

'Thanks for the offer, but I'm really tired tonight. It's been a long day,' she excused, thinking, no way, I'm not ready for that. 'A long few days, in fact. I doubt I'd be very good company.'

'Whatever suits you.' Alejandro didn't seem bothered as he shrugged and smiled, and for a moment she was tempted to accept his offer. Thankfully, reason prevailed. She'd be in his car, under his control, going who knew where. Alejandro might have been Tom's best friend, but she didn't know him from Adam. Would she break the habit of a lifetime, and climb into a stranger's car?

'Why don't we come to this fresh in the morning?' she suggested. 'We could meet at the café next door. I have a rehearsal at nine with my pianist, Jason. Shall we say eleven o'clock? That would suit me,' she couldn't resist adding with the faintest of edges.

One sweeping ebony brow lifted in acknowledgement of her counter-punch. If Alejandro's firm mouth hadn't been quite so dangerous when it curved like that, or his stare so amused and compelling, she might have turned on her heel and left him right then and there, but this change in him, from the stern individual at the dreadful reading of the will to the Master of the Sexual Universe, lounging in a club, was so surprisingly marked that curiosity got the better of her, and she waited to hear what he had to say next.

'What if I tell you that this can't wait until tomorrow?' he suggested.

'I'd say, you need to learn patience,' she countered levelly.

His brow shot up again, but this time the amusement had died in his eyes. Too bad. She had no intention of becoming anyone's doormat.

'Before you go,' he said, 'I want you to know that I really enjoyed your singing tonight. You are an exceptionally talented singer.'

She said simply, 'Thank you,' just as her singing teacher had advised when praise made Sienna feel awkward.

'Until tomorrow?' Alejandro queried.

She must have looked at him with a blank stare, because he reminded her about their next appointment at the coffee shop. 'Right,' she agreed, wondering with concern what exactly she was agreeing to. 'See you then...'

Dragging greedily on the chill night air, she didn't turn to see Alejandro had followed her out of the club. It was a relief to find her usual cab waiting at the kerb. She remembered very little of the drive home, and must have been in a state of shock, she concluded on her return. What would have happened if she had allowed Alejandro to take her home? Nothing, she rea-

soned sensibly as she put her key in the front
door. She was hardly his type. Coffee the next
morning in a bustling café was neutral territory,
and that was where they would sort things out.

Over a flat white? Did that seem likely?

A restless night later, concealer was needed
under her eyes. She was groggy and under par
at rehearsal, and Jason was kind not to mention it. 'See you tonight.' She forced a grin as
she hurried away to keep her date with destiny.

Her date with a flat white and a spoonful of
sugar, Sienna corrected herself firmly.

Arriving first, he ordered, then found a table.
A basket of pastries, coffee and a jug of hot
milk were duly delivered with early-morning
speed. Sienna breezed in, stared around—not
anxiously, but with a keen eye. He raised a hand
in greeting, and she wove her way through the
tables towards him. Not for the first time, he
wished they'd met under different circumstances, with no restrictions placed on him by
her brother, so they could proceed from casual
hook-up to bed. He wasn't proud of his attitude
towards sex. That was just how it was for him.
Sex was as essential as eating and sleeping. No
long-term commitment required, either by him
or the women he dated.

Sienna sat across the table, her knees a whisper away from his. 'Flat white?' She sounded pleased. 'How did you know?'

'Educated guess. Actually,' he admitted with a shrug, 'Tom told me about your love of strong coffee with just a hint of steamed milk.'

'Tom loved strong coffee, straight up,' she remembered with a wistful smile that drew his attention to her lips. 'Oh, and by the way, good morning, Alejandro,' she added with a smile into his eyes. 'Where would you like to begin your interrogation?'

His mock-warning look made her blush. Where he'd like to begin was better kept to himself, so he confined himself to the blandest of questions, if only to see her kissable mouth form the syllables. 'I hope your rehearsal went well this morning?'

'Very well, thank you.'

'You sang great last night. I trust you got home safely?'

Holding his gaze, she barely missed a beat. 'Of course, I did. I made sure of it, didn't I?'

'I can't imagine what you're suggesting, *señorita*.'

'Can't you?' she said with a teasing sceptical look.

Neither one of them was a pushover, and that pleased him, for some reason. 'Have you had a chance to give any thought to your plans for the land you have inherited?'

'Launch straight in, why don't you?' Her eyes sparkled with amusement, challenge and warning as she stared at him over the rim of her coffee cup.

'You might be relieved to hear I can find a way out of this.'

'And what's that?' Putting her cup down, she frowned.

'I buy the land, and set you free.'

Pulling her head back, she gave him a caustic look. 'Not a chance, *señor*. What makes you think I'd ever want to sell that land? And I certainly don't need to be set free, by you or anyone else.'

'Caring effectively for so much land is a huge responsibility.'

'Here ends today's sermon?' she intoned, clearly not afraid of mocking him, but her expression quickly changed to serious. 'Do you think I don't know that?'

Sitting back, she contemplated the table for a moment or two, before lifting her chin to accuse him of leaping to conclusions. 'By your own admission, you know nothing about me, yet you've decided I'm not capable of handling responsibility.'

'That's not what I said,' he defended. 'But I

don't believe you have any experience of land management. I'm quite prepared to discuss this issue in more detail, back at my place—'

'We can discuss it here,' she cut in firmly.

'Where it's noisy and hardly private? I give you my word, you can leave at any time, and I won't pressure you to act one way or another. All I ask is that you hear me out before firming up any decision.'

Going on Sienna's past reaction to his invitations, he fully expected her to say no, but instead she stood and said with a shrug, 'Okay.'

He led the way out of the café, en route to the next chapter in the ongoing saga of Acosta versus Slater, and, for once, he couldn't wait to turn the page.

The last time she'd been to Alejandro's smart London home, she had arrived on foot. This was very different. He kept the sleek red sports car, in which they'd arrived, in an underground garage beneath the house, where it joined a line of similar supercars. Alejandro got out first, and came around to open her door. Good start. An elevator took them up to the main part of the house. Its doors slid open to reveal a subtly lit corridor where the décor was opulent and subdued, and jewel colours predominated. Her feet were instantly encased in deep-pile carpet. Full sensory overload. She dragged deep on the scent of old money. But new ideas, she hoped.

She gave a sharp intake of breath when Alejandro put his hand on her shoulder. 'Apologies,' he murmured. 'I didn't mean to startle you. Just leading you in the right direction.'

She could only hope.

His touch lingered, not in actual fact, but in her muscle memory. It was so compelling. He was so compelling. So, keep your wits about you. But it was hard not to be beguiled by so much hypnotic glamour.

That same glamour was reflected in Alejandro's house. Gilt-framed mirrors and oil paintings of horses lined the corridor, together with impressive bowls and urns with an oriental look about them. No children allowed here, she thought with amusement. How did he cope when the children of his brothers and sister visited, when everything had obviously been curated to impress? But not by Alejandro, Sienna suspected. The *objets d'art* had been placed to impress a man who was clearly oblivious to his surroundings. Alejandro had probably paid someone a fortune to come and mess up his house. If she lived here, there'd be clean lines and no clutter. But she didn't live here, so...

'What are you thinking?' Alejandro asked when she stopped walking to stare around.

'That I've left my world behind and entered yours.'

He remained non-committal. Had he brought her here to try to seduce her? No. Alejandro was far too cool for that. The more pressing question was, if he tried, did she have what it took to resist him?

Thankfully, he gave her no chance to think about it, before opening a polished mahogany door she remembered well, because it led into his study.

CHAPTER FOUR

BLUEBEARD'S LAIR, this was not, though it was the same sombre room she remembered from the reading of Tom's will. In that moment she felt sorry for Alejandro. With all his money, he should have someone to help him brighten up his life. Even a coat of whitewash would be better than these dull grey walls.

'Would you mind if we went somewhere else?' she asked as a shiver of recall crept down her spine.

'The will, of course,' he said, remembering. 'I'm sorry, I should have been more sensitive.'

Was it too much to hope they were getting somewhere at last?

'How about the library?' he suggested.

Just the word lifted her spirits. 'Perfect.'

And it was. Who owned so many books, apart from Alejandro? Some were clearly very old and precious. There was even a beautifully illuminated manuscript in glass case.

'You're a very lucky man...'

For a while, she was so immersed in studying Alejandro's books, she almost forgot the purpose of her visit. There was so much to look at—and he had so much to explain. Halting her avid tour, she turned around to face him. 'What was it you wanted to say to me? I should tell you right away that my half of the island is not for sale.'

'What a relief,' he intoned dryly. 'Why don't you sit down?'

'Will this take long?'

'Why? Do you have another rehearsal?'

It would have been the easiest thing in the world to say yes, but she couldn't lie to him. 'No. I'm free for the rest of the day,' she admitted.

'Then, relax,' he advised. 'Better we get to know each other if we're going to work through this successfully.'

Tipping her chin, she gave him a look. 'I'll tell my lawyer what you said.'

'Your lawyer?'

It had been an off-the-cuff remark, but Alejandro's face had changed completely, from open and easy, to narrow-eyed suspicion. 'That was a joke. Not a very good one,' she conceded, but the storm in his eyes failed to subside. He must think she was a gold-digger with only one thought on her mind—to do as she pleased, when she pleased, and to hell with him. 'I'm sorry. It was an ill-judged remark. If the land's worth that much to you—'

Alejandro shot back with passion. 'Of course, it is. I care deeply about the land and the people who have lived there all their lives. Their livelihoods and future depend on careful management, and I won't see anything stand in the way of that.'

'Are you suggesting I'd do something to harm them?'

'I don't know what you'd do,' he admitted as things grew heated. 'I don't know you.'

'That makes two of us, but, whether you believe me or not, this isn't about money for me.'

'It must be the only thing on God's earth that isn't,' he said with a scowl.

Perhaps suspicion always accompanied great wealth, and again she felt sorry for Alejandro. Could he trust anyone when so much was at stake? 'I apologise for wasting your time,' she said, standing. 'To be honest, I don't know yet what I'm going to do with Tom's land. But—'

'But you must have some idea,' he cut in.

'All I can promise is that you have my word that I will do everything in my power to protect that land.'

Laying out her hopes and dreams in any more

detail, before Alejandro, a man with boundless power, and teams of people to do his bidding, would make her own ideas seem naïve and unformed. She didn't have a business plan, or even an architect's sketch to show him. All she had was a firm conviction that she would build a tribute to Tom. Telling Alejandro that she would make that happen somehow would only make her look foolish. He'd think she was a dreamer, or, worse, he might imagine that she was hoping to lean on him to bring her dreams to fruition.

'I imagine you won't be doing anything in the near future, unless you have the money to proceed,' he said in a clipped tone.

Why didn't he just come right out and say it: before she got her hands on Tom's money? Alejandro had reinforced the fact that she'd have to ask him to release funds from Tom's estate to do anything, and even then he'd be looking over her shoulder every step of the way. They couldn't go on like this, facing each other, daggers drawn like two combatants in a ring. 'You know music's my first love—'

He pounced on that one simple statement. 'Are you planning to open a music school on the island?'

'Is that such a terrible idea?'

To her relief, Alejandro appeared to relax. 'I'd be concerned that you'd find enough pupils on a small island to keep the school afloat, and I'd have to wonder why you didn't open your school in London.'

Sienna had been wondering the very same thing, but the mysterious island that Tom had loved so much beckoned to her. Tom had shouldered the responsibility of bringing her up, and had allowed Sienna to pursue her dreams at music college. It seemed only right to try to repay him, and where better to build a retreat than the sun-kissed land Tom had loved so much, with all the associated health benefits the island could bring to those who needed it?

'Don't forget your bag when you go.'

Jerked back into the present, she remembered that Alejandro had offered to take her home whenever she wanted. 'I won't—and thanks for the lift. It's very kind of you.'

'Under the circumstances?' he suggested.

She found a smile. 'Let's just say, I appreciate the kindness.'

Alejandro Acosta could say more with his eyes than anyone she knew could with words, and his gaze right now said, don't mock me.

I won't, she answered silently on her way to the door.

Everything went well until they brushed against each other when he opened the door, and then, like two magnets that couldn't fend off contact for ever, they exchanged a brief, intense stare. For a moment, she was sure he was going to kiss her.

Should have known better, Sienna ruefully accepted as Alejandro stepped back. He was a seasoned campaigner, while she was very new to the game.

'We'll talk again tomorrow,' he said, 'but, if you'll take some advice, don't make any decisions until you've seen the land.'

'I won't,' she promised on her way across the hall.

'I'm looking forward to hearing you sing again,' Alejandro said, surprising her.

'Glutton for punishment?' she suggested.

'Glutton for pleasure,' he countered with another of his disturbing looks.

Apart from a few civilities, they didn't speak as he drove her home, but Alejandro so close beside her heightened her senses to a painful degree. The instant she closed the door on her bedsit, she touched her lips with her fingertips, imagining the warm pressure of his lips on her mouth. A restless night followed, and it felt as if she'd only just dozed off, but light was streaming through the curtains when the phone rang. 'Hello,' she managed groggily, fumbling the receiver.

'I'm taking you home from the club tonight, okay?'

'Alejandro?' Instantly awake, she shot up in bed. 'Do you always firm up your plans before other people are properly awake?'

'Best time ever,' he countered in an amused drawl. 'How do you think I'm so successful in business?'

'No scruples?' she suggested dryly.

'Harsh,' he said, but his tone was disturbingly intimate, and the smile in his voice warmed her.

Sienna gave a spectacular performance that night. Not wanting to crowd her, he waited at the stage door, mingling with a group of fans for the sheer pleasure of hearing them praise her. Finding time for everyone, Sienna laughed, signed autographs and shared her joy. Her gaze found him right away, but he shook his head, indicating that she should carry on for as long as she needed to.

He took her to a small supper club off Regent Street where the waiters were discreet, the clientele was low-key classy and the crème brulée was spectacular. They laughed when he told her it was something she shouldn't miss.

'Are you trying to bribe me with burned sugar and cream?' she suggested, cocking her head to one side so her eyes sparkled in the candlelight like emeralds.

'I'm recommending something I know you'll enjoy.'

'In that case...' She smiled up at the waiter. 'Two crème brulées, please.'

He never ate pudding, but tonight he'd make an exception.

They talked about everything except the land. It was hard not to enjoy talking about the exceptional childhoods both of them had been lucky enough to experience. They made no mention of the tragedy that had struck both their families, and it seemed as if their mellow surroundings had provided a cocoon, where they could enjoy each other's company without the harsh facts of life intruding. Against all the odds, he realised as Sienna sucked sugar cream from her tiny spoon. Even he couldn't see much wrong with that. 'Coffee?' he suggested.

'No, thanks. I don't like decaf, and I wouldn't be able to sleep if I drank full-strength.'

Her innocence pierced him. He couldn't think of any other woman who'd have sleep at the front of her mind right now. 'Mint tea? Anything at all?'

'No, thank you. I've really enjoyed tonight,' she said, as if she was as surprised as he was. 'I haven't felt so relaxed in ages, even though we've been talking about our childhoods, which usually makes me sad.'

'But it also drives you on, doesn't it?' he proposed with a frown. 'I mean, we both like to seize the moment, seize life, and squeeze every drop out of it, because of everything we've lost.'

'I've never looked at it like that,' she admitted.

'It's hard to see the positives, when they come with so much grief attached.'

'And wariness,' she added with a twisted smile.

'And that,' he conceded as he called for the bill, and stood to pull back her chair.

When she turned their faces were briefly so close, they shared the same breath, the same air. Something changed between them then. Whether it was the adrenalin of performance in her case, or the thrill of the hunt in his, he had no idea, but Sienna's eyes had darkened as she stared into his, tightening his groin to the point of pain. *Behave,* he told himself sternly. He'd take her straight home. That was the right thing to do.

But the right thing to do was never the only option, and without giving it too much thought he turned the vehicle in the direction of Mayfair. Sienna didn't query the route. Tension spiked between them. *Sorry, Tom.* They both knew why they were here, he reflected as he turned the wheel and they parked up in his underground garage.

He called the elevator, and they stepped inside. It stopped suddenly between floors. Had Sienna leaned back against the controls on purpose? Or was fate in charge? It really didn't matter. Neither did who made the first move. Fire raged equally between them.

'Take me to bed,' she whispered.

Was Sienna fulfilling some long-suppressed desire? Was he? Probably. Did it matter? They could have been standing on a beach, or lying on a bed entwined around each other, and there would still be this same, undeniable urge to forget the past and put the future on hold for now.

How she arrived in Alejandro's bedroom would always remain a bit of a blur. She remembered them tearing at each other's clothes as the same erotic force swept them into its embrace. It was only when Alejandro had removed the last vestige of her clothing that she realised how calm he had become, while she was still wild for him. He'd made her feel safe enough to lose all her inhibitions. She was lucky that this man, who so closely resembled a barbarian, quickly proved he could be measured too. It was a surprise to find his control really turned her on.

'Do you want me?' he murmured, knowing

what her answer would be. She had no breath to tell him, *So much.*

Answering his every touch with frantic sounds of need, she grabbed at this chance to put the past with all its sadness behind her. They were communicating on the most basic level: touch, taste, scent, and sound. Alejandro's strength and her need combined into one irresistible force. Impossibly attractive, virile and masculine, he made it impossible to hold back, and why should she? Plunging into a powerful release when he'd barely touched her, she screamed out, *'Yes!'* as the pleasure waves consumed her.

'Greedy...' Alejandro murmured, smiling against her mouth when she was calm enough to hear him.

'Are you complaining?'

'Complaining?' he said softly. 'No...'

And then he kissed her again, while she writhed shamelessly in his grasp.

'Slow down,' he advised in the same soothing tone. 'We've got all night.'

But she was trembling with arousal and was soon on the brink again. Alejandro knew exactly how to school her responses, and he made her wait.

'Brute,' she complained, pummelling him with frustration. 'I'm not one of your world-class ponies to be trained in your ways.'

'No,' he agreed. 'You're far more wilful, so your schooling may take a lot longer.'

She could only hope. Loving the way he held her so lightly, yet so firmly, always keeping satisfaction at bay, raising her arousal to a thrilling breaking point. Pinning her wrists above her head, he continued the delicious torture, leaving her whimpering with desire as he laved her nipples until she thrust and bucked with longing. But, once again, he pulled back.

Calling him names she couldn't believe she knew, she gasped with relief when she realised that Alejandro wasn't stopping, he was protecting them both.

Easing her legs apart, he allowed the tip of his erection to brush against her most sensitive core. Placing a hand beneath her buttocks, he lifted her. Slipping a pillow beneath her hips, he positioned her to his liking. Drawing her knees back, she wrapped her legs around his waist. Exposed and vulnerable, she had never felt so safe. Arching her back, she cried out with need, but still he refused to be rushed.

Well, she refused to be kept waiting.

But could she take him? Could she take all of him? She had to. This was the oblivion she needed. Alejandro was everything she needed. And more.

CHAPTER FIVE

SIENNA WAS BEAUTIFUL. Her pleasure was his pleasure. Drawing sensation out was a skill he took seriously. By the time he eased her over the edge again, she had reached another level of consciousness. Denial followed by fulfilment allowed her to experience the ultimate in arousal, and she came with his very first thrust.

They both needed this, he reasoned as he moved rhythmically and firmly. He allowed her to use him, exactly as she wished. Having extracted every last pulse of pleasure, he was careful not to over-stimulate her recovering body, but remained confident that it wouldn't be long before Sienna was desperate for more.

'If you'd like me to stop,' he teased as she clung to him.

She turned a fierce stare on his face. 'Don't you dare!'

'Whatever you say, *señorita*—'

'You'll give me everything I want?' she queried.

In bed? Yes, of course he would. Out of bed remained to be seen.

It was easy to stir her hunger again with shallow, teasing probes. Sienna encouraged him with words he doubted she'd used before. 'I can do that,' he whispered against her ear. 'And I'll keep on doing it, until you ask me to stop.'

'That's never going to happen,' she assured him fiercely.

By rotating his hips, he could massage the little nub that begged for his attention. Persuasive brushes and nudges were gradually turned into a firmer movement that had her teetering on the edge. He held off for as long as he could, while Sienna gripped his buttocks with fingers turned to steel.

'Relax...let me do this,' he instructed, and once she was limp again he used firm, rhythmical strokes to bring her the pleasure she craved.

It was light when she woke in Alejandro's bed, taking stock of a body well used. He was already out of bed—and dressed. For the office?

'Hey,' he urged, seeing she was awake. 'I've got work to do. Do we need to talk before I go?'

That did it. She was instantly awake. And offended. 'Don't let me keep you.'

'I've got meetings crowding in on me, babe.'

Babe? 'You don't have to explain. Just go.'

Alejandro looked relieved. Throwing back the curtains, he blinded her with light. 'Take as long as you need,' he said. 'There's no point in rushing. The staff won't be back until midday.'

By which time, she must be gone, Sienna gathered, reading between the lines. Hot shame suffused her. Alejandro was treating her like a one-night stand. Not that there was anything wrong with a one-night stand, but she had thought they had more between them.

Wrong. He was clearly having second thoughts about sleeping with her. But at the restaurant last night she'd thought they'd become close. Wrong again. Alejandro was merely being polite. She wasn't his type, and she should never have pushed things until they ended up like this. Her cheeks flared red when she remembered launching herself at him in the elevator—but he'd done quite a bit of launching too. Okay, but she should have resisted.

Seriously?

Whatever their motivation, sex without emotion would never be enough, Sienna realised as Alejandro strode to the door. She'd never really considered what she wanted, or even what she expected, from relationships before. A craving for the closeness her parents had shared, she supposed, biting back emotion, and yet, there was always that fear that caring too much could lead to the most terrible loss. Both she and Alejandro wore armour to protect against that.

So, where did that leave her? Having woken content in the certainty that they'd built on their closeness last night, she now suspected that Alejandro had been having sex, while she had expected too much from him on the emotional front. Like supreme athletes, they'd given an outstanding display, satisfying their most basic needs, but to read anything more than that into what they'd done was foolish. A night that had meant so much to her, a night when she'd fooled herself into believing that concord of mind led to intimacy of body, had ended now, and as abruptly as a safety curtain coming down on a show.

Some show, she mused with an ironic twist of her mouth. 'Don't worry, Alejandro, I'll be leaving soon.'

Quite suddenly, her nakedness became an embarrassment, and she dragged the sheet close around her body before she got out of bed. 'Do you mind if I take a quick shower before I go?'

'Of course. Be my guest.'

That just about summed it up, Sienna thought as Alejandro palmed his keys. She was a chance visitor, no more than that, and, as if to prove it, he didn't look back once as he left the room.

* * *

Had he been too harsh? No. He had no intention of taking things further, and it would be wrong to lead Sienna on. He shouldn't have seduced her in the first place.

Seduced her? Desire had been mutual. Maybe, but nothing lasted for ever, and beneath Sienna's bravado she was vulnerable, and he would not stamp on that.

In spite of this reasoning, on the drive to his office he could think of nothing but Sienna. She'd woken in obvious confusion: where was she? What had they done? When realisation had dawned, her fantasies had taken over: they'd made love. Seeing her so happy, he'd felt an impulse to stay with her. Sleep-rumpled, and flushed, she had never looked more beautiful to him, but his world turned relentlessly, and he had no doubt that, when Sienna thought things through, she'd be glad that he'd gone.

Flashbacks of the previous night plagued him throughout the morning. It was hard not to smile when he remembered the little anecdotes they'd shared during their meal in the restaurant. There was no doubt that, on a personal level, they'd got on really well. As far as sex was concerned, her passion had surprised him. But he should have known better—

It was almost a relief to answer his secretary's

call on the intercom, but before he could say a word, there was a knock at the door. 'Come.'

Anticipating the arrival of his morning coffee, he had already turned back to the documents on his desk.

'Sorry—this couldn't wait—'

'Sienna!' He was on his feet immediately. 'Is something wrong?'

'I hope I'm not interrupting anything?'

'Nothing that can't wait,' he assured her. 'Come in. Close the door. I'll ask June to bring us some coffee.'

'Don't.'

His anxiety levels soared when he saw the expression on her face. 'I insist you come in and sit down.' Crossing the room in a couple of strides, he closed the door behind her, and then returned to the desk, where he pulled out a chair. 'Sit down and tell me what's on your mind.'

'You promised we'd talk, and we didn't,' she said.

'That's it?' he queried as he propped one hip against the polished wood surface.

'Should there be more?'

She seemed tense. Wanting to make her feel at ease, he pulled out a chair to face hers. Big mistake. Now he couldn't concentrate on anything but her scent rolling over him: wildflower and soap. She'd twisted up her glorious hair, which revealed the fine line of her cheek-bones—a pang hit him when he took in her shabby coat. No one in his office dressed like this. Quite suddenly the luxuries he took for granted seemed both superfluous and meaningless. 'Are you sure you're okay?' he asked with concern.

'I just wanted to talk,' she insisted. 'I promise, it won't take long.'

'Take as long as you want.' Lifting the phone, he issued a brief instruction: 'No calls.'

There was always a degree of awkwardness the day after first-time sex, but this had never happened to him before. He was worried if Sienna was hurt, if she'd had second thoughts. 'Are you hungry?' he asked, hoping to break the tension. 'I can send out for breakfast—or we can find a café—'

'No,' she cut in. 'No more distractions, Alejandro. I'm fine as I am.'

'If it's the land you're worried about, don't be. I'm happy to revise my offer—'

'I'm sorry?' she said quietly, frowning.

'The land,' he repeated, following this with a figure well over the land's value, which would enable Sienna to fulfil all her dreams. He imagined Tom would want this. Withholding Sienna's money just didn't seem right to him.

'I knew I shouldn't have come here,' she murmured, as if speaking her thoughts out loud.

'Why?' Who on this fine earth had access to the amount of money he'd offered? Tom's legacy paled into insignificance by comparison with the sum he'd suggested for Sienna's land.

She studied him thoughtfully. 'I've been wondering, since I woke up this morning, how amazing sex with someone I think I could really care about could leave me with such an empty feeling, but now I know.'

Her words hit him like bullets. Why was she so upset? Sienna had seemed to enjoy last night every bit as much as he had. 'I think you'd better explain.'

'I'm happy to,' she assured him. Lifting her chin, she let him have it straight. 'Having softened me up with fabulous sex, you're now putting forward the most ridiculous pay-off.'

'Is that what you think this is?'

'What else am I supposed to think? You got what you wanted,' she said with a shrug, 'while I got what I thought I wanted.'

'So, you didn't...want it?' he pressed, drawing his head back in bemusement as he remembered Sienna's passionate responses.

'At the time? Absolutely,' she confirmed.

'Now?' Her eyes turned sad.

He understood from this that any thought

of sex must be returned to Pandora's box and safely sealed inside. That left one thing to talk about. 'You'll have total autonomy over the proceeds of the sale. You'll get the money immediately. No coming to me, cap in hand. You can do anything you want with the money. Please,' he said when Sienna didn't seem to take this in, 'tell me what you want.'

She was silent for so long, he wondered if she'd forgotten the question, but then she said in the smallest of voices, 'All I want is my brother back.' *Dios.* Guilt crushed him.

'No amount of money can bring Tom back,' she added in the same faint tone. But then she rallied and pierced him with an accusing stare. 'And your money can't buy my respect.'

'I'm not trying to buy your respect,' he defended.

'Then, don't offer me money. Why can't you understand, Alejandro? If you have children one day, are you going to teach them that money can buy anything and everything? Would you still do that, knowing it's a lie?'

Impassioned, she sprang up. He stood too. 'If this is because of last night, don't you think it's time we were honest with each other, Sienna? We both wanted sex. The decisions we made were entirely mutual.'

'Decisions?' Her laugh sounded ugly in the

pristine surroundings of his large, light-filled office. 'Our bodies took all the decisions, leaving you and me out of it. Neither one of us made anything close to a rational decision last night.'

'Are you saying that you regret what happened?'

'Let me think about this,' she flared. 'You left before I was properly awake, as if sex was nothing more to you than a mechanical act.'

'It's only natural, when emotions are heightened, that instinct takes over.'

'Instinct?' she queried. 'That just about sums it up. What about emotion, Alejandro?'

'Says you?' he countered. 'Accusing me of trying to pay you off, you couldn't be further from the truth. I'm offering you a bank draft that will allow you to pay off all your debts, and more besides—'

'What do you know about my debts?' she cut across him angrily.

Did she really think he wouldn't do his homework? How could he make Sienna understand how careful he had to be, with so much at stake? 'I'm not trying to buy you off. I'm making you a more than fair offer for the land that will allow you to do anything you choose to do for the rest of your life.'

Thrusting her face towards him, she exclaimed furiously, 'But isn't buying me off exactly what this is? Or do you make a habit of giving away so much money on a whim?'

'There's no whim involved,' he fired back. 'I'll do anything it takes to get Tom's land under safe management.'

'D'you seriously think I'd do anything to damage Tom's land?'

'That's the whole point. Until you tell me your plans, I don't know what you intend to do.'

'Okay…' She took a deep breath, and a very long moment before admitting, 'Maybe I shouldn't have sounded off, but it takes a lot to come to someone like you and expose my hopes and dreams, when I know I can never compete with your resources.'

'Go on,' he encouraged.

'You and Tom shared an island, and now Tom's share belongs to me. I would never embark on something I don't know anything about without consulting someone who does. That doesn't mean I won't make my own decisions when I have all the information to hand, but what about this—what if I lease the land I don't use to you?'

That was a novel thought, and one that hadn't occurred to him, he was forced to admit, but there were still problems, even with that proposal. 'I need to know what you're going to do with the land you keep.'

'Anything I like, sure—bearing in mind that you have my promise not to do anything that might be to the detriment of the land, or the people living on it.'

'Will you build a music school?'

Lifting her chin, she explained, 'I'm hoping to build a music therapy centre in memory of Tom.'

The fact that they had such similar plans shouldn't have surprised him. They had both loved Tom, and what better to do with the money Tom had left than to create a facility in his name, to help those who were suffering as Tom had?

'Music has the power to heal,' Sienna continued with compelling sincerity. 'That isn't just something I believe. I've seen it in action.'

As had he, he recollected, when he'd heard Sienna sing. For that short time, he had been transported, and uplifted, a state, he was forced to admit, that was entirely new to him.

'I can tell you one thing,' she said with a direct stare. 'That land will never be for sale.'

Pulling his head back, he stared at Sienna. He always took the lead in business and had never known a fair offer to be refused. Nothing like this had ever happened to him before, but, far from angering him, she intrigued him.

'You may change your mind,' he thought it only fair to remind her.

'And I may not,' she said.

'This has nothing to do with last night, does it?' he pressed, frowning.

'Everything between us is, or should be, connected to the land,' she said with renewed intent that was somehow unconvincing. 'Anything personal shouldn't even be entering our thinking,' she continued in the same vein. 'We wouldn't have met, if it hadn't been for Tom, and you should know by now that I'm not impressed by wealth, or power, or influence. I've managed to jump through quite a few hoops in the past, and I can do so again.'

'Sienna, wait.'

He sprang to his feet as she made for the door, but her step didn't falter and, like their first meeting in London, he was left alone, listening to the sound of her footsteps fading.

For a few moments he did nothing, then he returned to the desk and called his PA to make arrangements to leave the country. He and Sienna needed space from each other. Thanking his control for allowing him to make this decision, he resisted the impulse to go after her.

A woman removing herself from his life was new to him, but it held faint echoes of previous loss, and for that alone he knew he'd made the right decision. But it was hard to cut off Sienna completely, though it seemed incredible that a woman who aggravated and attracted him in equal measure could have this hold over him. Because she lifted him with her singing, he reasoned, and that made him feel light. She made him laugh, when no one else could, and last night he had almost believed that she completed him.

All the more reason not to drag things out. Tom's loss had reminded him that risk never passed, and pain could rarely be eased. Maybe he could have handled things better with Sienna. He hadn't set out to hurt her.

And now a bland and boring world loomed without her?

So, he'd fill that gap with business. They'd meet up eventually, if only to agree on the land. These thoughts were perfectly logical, but that didn't help where his preoccupation with Sienna was concerned. Two strong people, who'd grown accustomed to paddling their own canoe, were probably both wondering right now if a satisfactory resolution between them was even possible.

Was he going to sit around, doing nothing, waiting to find out? No. He would fly to the island, making the break with Sienna, for her sake, as much as for his.

CHAPTER SIX

SHE WAS PREGNANT.

Six weeks had passed since she'd last seen Alejandro, and now she knew for sure.

Expecting a baby changed everything. Absolutely everything. The growing suspicion that she was no longer alone in her body had just received the most amazing proof positive in the form of two horizontal blue lines. She'd done the test three times in the tiny staff bathroom at the club, to make sure. There was no mistake.

How could it be? They'd used protection.

Protection can fail. How many times had she been told that back at school?

How could it not be? Staring into the mirror, she was overwhelmed by feelings of elation: a child, their child, a new life, a new love, an arrow to send flying out into the world.

She was pregnant with Alejandro's baby. By mutual agreement, they'd gone their separate ways for now—at the worst time possible, as it turned out. But nothing could spoil the moment. If she could give their child half the love her own mother had shown her, their baby would be the happiest child on earth. With every fibre of her being, she welcomed this new life. This baby was a living extension of the families they'd lost.

Thinking about her mother always made her pause, and always made tears threaten, but this was such a special moment, if her parents had lived to see it Sienna knew they'd be rejoicing and would surely tell Sienna that regret had no part to play.

Pregnancy tests were so precise they even showed the approximate date of conception. Six-plus weeks. Her cheeks flushed red at the memory. Yes, they'd used protection, but with passion like theirs anything could happen.

Alejandro.

Eyes closed, heart open, she knew for certain, only him...only ever could be him.

'Welcome, little one.' Mapping her still-flat stomach, she smiled gently as happiness flooded through her. 'Sleep and grow strong. You don't have anything to worry about. I'm here for you.'

Sienna felt as if she were walking on air as she crossed the deserted club to join Jason in rehearsal at the piano. Alejandro's baby had brought everything into clearer, brighter focus, making her world spin on a completely different axis. All those years of determinedly feeling nothing had vanished in an instant, as if the most wonderful switch had been turned on.

Would a child change Alejandro in the same way?

How would he react? She was desperate to tell him, but he'd left the country, his PA had informed her when she'd rung. The woman had politely refused to hand over Alejandro's personal details. Would she pass on a message? 'Señor Acosta can always contact you at the club, should he wish to do so.' Those cold words had chilled Sienna—

'Hey, Sienna—daydreaming this morning?'

With a smile of apology, she said hi to Jason.

'I see our friend is back.'

'Our friend?' she queried.

'Alejandro Acosta,' Jason explained. 'His superyacht has returned to the Thames.'

Apprehension, panic and excitement roiled inside her. She could tell him her news. Today! The instant the rehearsal was over, she'd go straight to his yacht, and—

What if his security staff wouldn't allow her on board? She'd sit on the dock and wait until they did.

She turned as the manager of the club shouted

to her from the doorway of his office. 'Hey, Sienna, call for you.' Her heart thundered a tattoo. But surely it wouldn't be *him*, would it?

'Take it,' Jason encouraged, seeing how tense she was. 'I'll still be here when you get back.'

Flashing a smile in Jason's direction, she hurried off to take the call.

'Hello?'

'Sienna?'

She almost jumped out of her skin. 'Alejandro? It is you. I was just thinking about you.'

'Good thoughts, or bad?'

His voice rolled over her like melted chocolate, and he sounded amused, not at all like the matter-of-fact businessman prowling his office. 'I'll leave you to decide,' she said, smiling.

'Why don't you come here, and tell me yourself?'

'Where are you?'

'At the coffee shop next door.'

Breath hitched in her throat at the thought of him just a few yards away.

'Are you still there?' he queried in a low, mellifluous drawl.

'I'm still here.' Gathering her wits quickly, she added his private number to the contacts on her phone.

'If you're too busy to join me for coffee…?'

'I'd love to join you.' Major understatement. 'Thank you.'

'See you in ten?'

'I'll have to—' Too late. The line had already cut.

Making her excuses to the manager, and then to Jason, she postponed the rehearsal.

'You don't have to explain to me,' Jason told her with a smile.

Alejandro's striking presence in the everyday surroundings of the local café had drawn everyone's attention, and he took her breath away. He stood as she approached and gave her a quick assessment. 'Good to see you, Sienna. You're looking well. The London drizzle obviously suits you.'

He suited her.

'Flat white? Something to eat? Are you okay? You usually have a lot to say for yourself. Did the cat get your tongue?'

'You're right about London suiting me,' she said, anxious not to give him the impression that she was nervous on this occasion. 'Nothing to eat, thank you,' she added as he pulled out her chair.

'A flat white, please,' he said to the waitress.

'It's good to see you again, Alejandro.' Another major understatement. Couldn't he just look ordinary for once? Must he command every space?

'It's good to be back—'

Her brain scrambled to find a reason for his visit. Why was Alejandro here? They'd made no progress with the land. She couldn't afford the air fare to Spain yet, though she was saving hard.

Don't flatter yourself that you're the reason he's here. He wants the land.

Did he? Well, he hadn't mentioned it yet. And where the baby was concerned, she had nothing to be ashamed of. The promise of new life was a reason for joy. If she would fight for the land Tom had left her, how much harder would she fight for her unborn child? *Their* unborn child, Sienna's ever-present conscience rushed to remind her.

'Don't let your coffee go cold...'

She'd made him suspicious. Alejandro was giving her a long, assessing look. Going through the motions of lifting the cup to her lips, she nursed it for a while, wondering if this was the right time to tell him. Putting the cup down again, she gave him a level stare. 'I'm glad you're here, there's so much I have to tell you.'

'I'm intrigued. But surely you don't want to tell me here?'

As he glanced around, she had to agree that

a bustling café was not the somewhere special she'd had in mind for when she told him about their baby.

He glanced at the door. 'Shall we go for a walk?'

'Why not?' she agreed, but even as they walked to the door, doubt crowded in. Could a man like Alejandro with his powerful engines running full tilt all the time, ever be able to slow that pace enough to accommodate a child? Or would he simply dump an obscene amount of money in her bank account and move on?

'I guess I should tell you why I'm really here,' he said as they sheltered beneath the awning.

Hope springs eternal wasn't just a saying, Sienna discovered as her pulse picked up pace. 'Yes?'

'I want you and Jason to perform at my party tomorrow night.'

For a few moments her brain refused to work, and then it computed: Alejandro was only here because he wanted to hire her to sing at his party tomorrow night. Get over it.

'Tomorrow?' she managed vaguely.

Any opportunity to sing was something she usually grabbed with both hands, but right now she felt achingly flat, because it was time to get real. Had she seriously imagined that the great Alejandro Acosta had found her so irresistible that he couldn't wait to see her again? She could see the headline now: *Billionaire Sleeps with Nightclub Singer and Both Live Happily Ever After.* This was just another deal for Alejandro. She and Jason were at the top of their game. It made sense for Alejandro to book them to entertain his guests.

And now doubts crowded in. 'Has someone dropped out last minute?'

Alejandro stared at her, perplexed. 'No,' he protested. 'I'd be very pleased if both you and Jason could perform at my party tomorrow night. You're the only act I want. It's that simple.'

Nothing was ever *that simple*. Whatever Alejandro wants he gets, sprang to mind. Her frown deepened as she remembered Alejandro's brusque PA, giving her the brush-off. Didn't he have a loyal army to arrange things like this?

'Will you do it, Sienna?' he pressed in a voice that was deep and compelling.

'I can't give you my answer until I've spoken to Jason.' But it would be a thrill to peer through the looking glass into another part of Alejandro's life. Plus, this would almost certainly be the best chance she'd get to tell him about their baby.

A more cautious side of Sienna urged her to stamp on the brakes and take a little time to get used to the fact that Alejandro was back. But he'd given her no time to consider at leisure, and caution lost out.

'Good. I'm glad that's settled,' he said with a dip of his head. 'And don't forget your passport.'

'My passport?' she queried with surprise.

'Standard procedure,' he explained. 'You'll have to go through security before either of you can board the yacht, and with time so short I'll need your answer today.'

'Will there be a fee?' she said, thinking of Jason.

Alejandro's outrageous offer made her blink. Was this another opportunity to stun her with his wealth? 'We won't need that much,' she protested, making a very much smaller counter offer.

'Don't you think you should check with Jason, before you turn down my proposed fee?'

Yes, she should, Sienna concluded, firming her jaw as she stared back at Alejandro. And she would, but even as she thought about Jason's likely reaction when he heard the amount they would be splitting between them a shiver of apprehension tracked down her spine. Alejandro had so much wealth and power. How would that affect the future, and their child? Would Alejandro even want to be a part of their lives?

'Jason will receive the same amount, of course.'

'What?' She stared at him blankly.

'You'll each receive—'

She didn't even hear the amount. Her brain had simply switched off. 'That's very generous of you,' she managed to mumble, knowing it would be wrong to rob Jason of the chance to make so much money for a single night's work. 'I'll let you know as soon as I've checked with Jason that we're both free.'

'I've already checked. Both of you are free.'

What else had Alejandro checked. Did he know she was pregnant? No. He'd have said something by now. Why hadn't she said something? And now it was too late. Alejandro was already lifting the collar of his jacket as he got ready to leave the shelter of the awning.

'Why don't you call Jason now?' he suggested.

'Good idea.' Fumbling for her phone, she almost dropped it, and gasped as he retrieved it and placed it back in her hand. Bare skin on bare skin was too, too much. 'Your yacht's at Tower Bridge?' she confirmed in an attempt to swerve her thoughts from skin-to-skin contact.

'Correct.'

There was only one notable yacht capable of stealing everyone's attention away from the historic bridge, and it was more of a floating palace than a boat.

'The *Acosta Dragon* is a convenient mode of transport.'

Laughter found its way through her concern. 'So's a bus,' she pointed out.

'Buses don't generally house Biedermeier pianos.'

That was a carrot Jason would find impossible to refuse, and Alejandro knew that. 'You have a Biedermeier piano on board?' she confirmed.

'Jason will love to play it, don't you think?'

'I'm sure he would, but he's not picking up the phone right now.'

'Then, try him later. And when you do speak to him, tell him that the piano used to belong to Clara Schumann, and that I've had it restored. It's such a beautiful instrument, it deserves to have someone like Jason at the keyboard.'

'Do you play?'

'A little. I find music both stimulating and relaxing, depending on my mood.'

What was Alejandro's mood now? she wondered, trying to read his eyes.

Braving the persistent drizzle, they started walking side by side. So close, and yet so far. No one seeing them would imagine they'd shared the most exciting passion, or that now they were expecting a child together. Seeing Alejandro again had reignited so many feelings. For such a long time, she'd believed it was easier not to feel, but now she longed for closeness, and for more openness in her life. She was the last of her family left, but soon there'd be one more. The tribe was coming back from the brink of extinction, and she owed it to her child to feel fully and experience everything keenly, both to honour her parents, and to live by her pledge that her child would be loved deeply and always, whatever the future held for Sienna and Alejandro.

'If you could perform around ten o'clock, that would be great,' Alejandro informed her as they prepared to cross the street and go their separate ways.

'*If* Jason can make it,' she reminded him.

'Jason will make it,' Alejandro said with confidence. 'Just tell him about the piano. A man like Jason doesn't play for money—or, at least, not just for money.'

'You're right,' she admitted. 'Jason would play for nothing, or even to an empty room. Same goes for me, which is probably why we're not rich and famous—'

'Like me?' Alejandro cut in.

'I didn't say that.' She glanced up into his harsh face, wondering what it would take to soften him.

'You didn't need to say it,' he assured her.

'Don't look so worried, Sienna. If I took offence that easily, I'd be reeling from verbal punches all the time.'

She pulled a face. 'I can't see you reeling any time, anywhere.'

'Thanks for the vote of confidence.'

'You're welcome,' she replied in the same dry tone, thinking that maybe, just maybe, they were reaching an accommodation where they could be friends, without the sex that had consumed them getting in the way. They'd reached the river and, like so many others before them, they stopped to take in the dazzling view. Even under a grey sky, the landscape of London was spectacular.

'Well, I'd better get going,' Alejandro said, turning in the direction of Tower Bridge.

'Wait—' She put a hand on his arm, which she quickly withdrew when he turned back to face her.

'Yes? Oh, yes, you had something you wanted to tell me.' Dipping his chin, he stared her in the eyes.

Suddenly, she was lost for words. She had intended to tell him about the baby, here, with this wonderful backdrop, but he was in a rush, and what she had to say couldn't be rushed.

'Sienna?'

Another question entirely forced its way through her lips. 'Can I ask you—about Tom?'

'Tom?'

'Yes,' she lied. How could she talk about a baby when even the sky was crying? But it was the perfect opportunity to talk about her brother—'If you've got time?'

'I'll make time.'

'It's just a question that's been plaguing me ever since the officers gave me the news of Tom's death. They said you brought him back from the battlefield. It meant so much to know he wasn't alone.' She could see that Alejandro neither sought praise, nor wanted it, and that he'd grown distant again.

'I've never left a comrade behind,' he admitted stiffly.

'I'm sure not.' She believed him absolutely.

'Tom,' he murmured, as if thinking back. 'There was no one like him. He could make us all laugh...'

There was something in Alejandro's eyes that said that wasn't the whole story. 'Go on,' she begged.

'Tom was the joker in the pack...'

'The troublemaker?' she asked with a frown.

'No,' Alejandro stated categorically, 'but Tom had his demons.'

After saying this, he pressed his lips together, as if he'd already said too much.

'I guess he covered any problems he had with humour?'

'Always,' Alejandro agreed.

'It can't have been easy for any of you,' she said with feeling.

'Which is why, when we were on leave, we played polo. Tom became quite the star.'

'I'm glad you had some good times together,' she said gently.

'We did.'

Alejandro's tone of voice said he didn't want to talk about it any more.

'You're drenched,' she said, thinking it would be a good time to part.

'And you need to take care of your voice. I need you in good shape tomorrow.'

'You're right.' She laughed as she huddled into her coat. 'I hope that both Jason and I can make it.'

'You will,' Alejandro stated with confidence.

With a wry smile, she hurried off.

Glancing over his shoulder at Sienna's fast-re-treating back, he made a promise to himself that Tom would be cloaked in sunlight for ever, as far as Sienna was concerned. It would crush her to know that her brother had been killed because he'd been reckless one time too many. Or that he'd put the lives of his comrades in terrible danger on that last night. Sienna had enough grief to deal with already.

He replayed their conversation over and over once he was back on the yacht, and knew, if he had needed further proof, that Tom's last few hours had impacted heavily on Sienna. Her eyes had filled with tears as she'd repeated what she'd been told, that Alejandro had held her brother in his arms, and spent that first long night with him, talking to Tom even though he'd gone. She'd been spared the disturbing details, and he was glad about that, but by the end of the telling something had changed in her voice, almost as if she found herself wishing for a different outcome. As if she'd never forget what he'd done for Tom, but would never forgive him for being the one who had lived.

Hearing Sienna praise his role in a nightmare when she only knew half the story cut him deep. Tom had been in one of his manic phases that night, convinced he could conquer the world, and had put the entire regiment in danger, several men being injured in the attempt to bring Tom back. Alejandro had succeeded with determination driving him on, and stayed by Tom's side. But he hadn't been able to save him, and that fact would stay with him for ever.

Wrenching his thoughts onto a lighter path, he was confident Sienna would delight his guests, even if, for once in his well-ordered life, his own thoughts regarding Sienna were in turmoil. Having decided to avoid her, he hadn't reckoned with Sienna lodging in his mind. At the forefront of his mind, in fact. He just couldn't get her out of his head. Perhaps her performance on his yacht would set things straight, proving once and for all that Sienna was nothing more than his last, fleeting connection with Tom.

Remembering her comment on the fee, he was glad to pay both Sienna and Jason a decent amount. For people who brought such enjoyment and peace of mind, it niggled him that musicians were always undervalued. Whatever Sienna imagined about coming to him cap in hand to ask for Tom's money, that situation would never sit easily with him. As far as he was concerned, Sienna and Jason were worth every penny of their fee.

Back in his stateroom, legs crossed, whisky in hand, he ruminated on the past few hours. Sienna didn't know what to make of him. That made two of them. With siblings, landholdings, and a business to protect, grief would have been a self-indulgent luxury when his parents were killed, and he had come to believe that he was impervious to pain. Like a wolf that depended on its strength, or the appearance of strength, for its survival, he had buried every vestige of emotion beneath a blizzard of activity that had made him richer than Croesus, but not as happy as his brothers and sister with their sometimes chaotic, but so obviously contented family lives.

He smiled as he glanced at the family photograph, and then grimaced as he thought about Tom. His friend's loss reminded him of how much pain it was possible to feel. For a man who valued control and self-control above everything else, he could not let that pain back in. Controlling both his experiences and his environment had always been his shield against pain. He was responsible for the livelihoods of many, many people, so taking himself off to grieve, or dwelling on anything overlong, would be an unforgivable self-indulgence—

The trilling of his phone jolted him back into the present. Glancing at the number, he allowed himself a smile. 'That's great news,' he told Sienna. 'I look forward to seeing you both tomorrow night.'

By the time he put the phone down, he knew she'd broken through his reserve. His capacity for feeling was back full force. There was no other way to explain his anticipation of their next meeting.

CHAPTER SEVEN

THIS MUST BE a dream, Sienna concluded as she struggled to take in the alternate, floating universe she was about to walk into with Jason. If her friend hadn't been at her side, she might have needed to pinch herself at the sight of so much unrestrained luxury.

Alejandro's sleek white yacht was enormous, easily the size of a low-rise upmarket building. It seemed incredible that, a few feet behind them, life went on as normal: pedestrians huddled in heavy coats as they hurried down the rain-slicked pavement, horns blared and engines revved, while ahead lay ordered calm. The soft strains of a jazz band filtered through the drizzle towards them, white lights twinkled with promise up on deck.

They were waiting to be checked off a guest list at the foot of the gangplank. Alejandro was right. They had to show their passports. His security guard loomed over them with a two-way radio in hand, checking their details. The guard's voice was curt, while his black-clad appearance was unrelentingly grim. After a few tense moments, he handed their passports back, and indicated that they were free to pass.

She had to tell herself that this was the adventure of a lifetime, before lifting her chin to walk the length of the sloping gangplank. Part of her was terrified, while another part was desperately eager to discover what type of world Alejandro inhabited when he wasn't residing in his sombre London house.

This is for you, Tom. This is me thanking your friend Alejandro for being with you at the end, and then all my debts to Alejandro are paid in full.

If only it were that easy, she reflected as her hand moved instinctively to map her still-flat stomach. Years of trying her hardest to feel nothing, because emotion hurt, and grief was corrosive, had to be put aside now because there was a new life inside her, and that child deserved a mother who confronted life with all its problems head-on.

A uniformed steward appeared seemingly out of nowhere with the offer to escort them to their quarters. There was no turning back now, Sienna concluded wryly as Jason murmured, 'Here we go,' adding discreetly, 'I don't know about you, Sienna, but I've no intention of missing a single second of this experience.'

Neither had she.

She was here.

Now he could relax.

Exhaling steadily, he pulled back from the rail. He'd sensed Sienna's arrival long before he'd caught sight of her. Call it intuition. Call it what the hell you liked. Almost an entire adult lifetime of suppressing feelings had been overturned by one infuriatingly unique woman. *Don't mess with my sister* was long in the past. He would never *mess* with Sienna. She wasn't any type of one-night stand, but a woman he was starting to admire for so many reasons, the way she stood up to him being just one. Sienna was also an outstanding musician, and he got the sense that there was so much more to learn about her.

And then there was lust.

He could think of little else but holding her in his arms again. Vulnerable, maybe, but she had her brother's stubborn side too. There was more steel in Sienna's character than even he had suspected. Not knowing her plans for the land was his main concern, but tonight was an opportunity to find out more. He had his own project planned for the island and would tolerate neither interference nor delay. She'd see reason when he explained. They'd come to an agreement soon.

And then?

Who knew what the future held? Once the deal was done, anything was possible. He'd miss the challenge of Sienna if she took his money, left and never came back. He'd miss the passion she brought to his bed. She was uniquely complex and endlessly intriguing—it was fair to say that Señorita Slater had turned his well-ordered world upside down.

Alejandro's yacht was like the most luxurious residence imaginable, as well as the most surprising. The first thing she noticed was how bright it was, and how full of colour. The overall impression of vitality and purpose was as different as could be from his austere London home.

The yacht was packed with elegant people, and she was surprised at how many smiled as she and Jason passed. There was a great atmosphere of ease and interest, and it was quite reassuring to notice that even these obviously well-heeled people were as awe-struck by their surroundings as Sienna.

There were new surprises around every corner, from the crystal staircase to the ice-topped bar, and she was agog at all the fabulous fashion and flashing jewels. She'd pitched her outfit about right, thank goodness. The understated floor-length column of emerald-green silk was a piece she'd been lucky enough to pick up for next to nothing in a trunk sale. Maybe it had been reduced, because it veered towards subtle, rather than obvious, but, whatever the case, she felt good.

The jazz band she'd caught a waft of on shore was even more impressive close up. As she'd suspected, when Alejandro mentioned that he played the piano, he was a cultured man who appreciated good music. Now she noticed the air of anticipation. She guessed it had nothing to do with the entertainment tonight, and everything to do with Alejandro. Everyone was waiting for him to appear, like the star of a show.

Thankfully, the rain had stopped falling, which allowed everyone to mingle on deck, but Sienna and Jason had no time to linger, as the officer escorting them was keen to show them to their rooms. He had explained that they would both have a stateroom for the night, where they could get ready for their performance. Refreshments would be provided, and they could call on the house phone for anything else they might need.

'How the other half live,' Jason murmured as they crossed the tastefully decorated reception lobby. Furnished in clean Scandi style, it was decorated with vibrant flower displays that gave the air a faint perfume. Modern art lent pops of colour to an already tasteful décor, and it was almost a let-down to step out onto the open deck, even in the shadow of the magnificent Tower Bridge.

'Welcome to the *Acosta Dragon*.'

She froze, then gazed up to see Alejandro watching them from an upper deck. Her entire body thrilled. Everything else faded into the background as Alejandro's potent charisma took over her world. Whatever they were, or weren't, to each other, his magnetism had enveloped her in a warm, erotic cloak.

'Thank you for inviting us,' she called up, trying to sound as if visiting a billionaire on his incredible yacht were something she did every day.

It was almost a relief when the officer invited them to follow him to their staterooms. She could do with a moment to accustom herself to the fact that Alejandro would be close for the rest of the night. Was he pleased to see her? It was hard to tell. His face had been in shadow. She replayed his voice in her mind. His tone had been warm, but he'd been greeting Jason too.

'Courage, mon brave,' Jason whispered, as if he read her uncertainty. 'You've got this.'

Had she? There was no doubt she could fulfil the terms of her contract to sing tonight, but just being here, on board Alejandro's mega-yacht, was a stark reminder of the power and wealth he wielded. Could she deal with Alejandro?

She had to, Sienna determined, for the sake of their child. He must agree to sharing the care of their baby. Surely, he would…

Snug in what turned out to be a gloriously opulent stateroom, she instructed herself firmly not to lose confidence, and to enjoy every moment of her time on board. The enormous fee she'd been paid was already safely stowed in her savings account, marked 'Tom's school', so she had every reason to be optimistic.

But…

But telling Alejandro about their child wouldn't be easy. How would he take the news? She allowed herself a moment of contemplation. Even the air smelled expensive, and although she lived more comfortably than many, Sienna couldn't change who she was. 'A nightclub singer?' had been directed at her more times than once, and not in a nice way. Could she bear it if Alejandro chose to dismiss her in the same way?

She'd have to. Toughing it out was her stock-in-trade. She and Alejandro had a child's future to consider, and anything else would be banished from her mind.

When she'd saved enough, she would visit the island—to find out what it had meant to Tom, if nothing else. The opportunity to build something exciting in his name filled her with enthusiasm for the future. How many times had she walked through the corridors of Tom's music centre in her mind? Airy classrooms, spacious practice rooms, and, of course, the Tom Slater Concert Hall had all come one step closer thanks to the massive fee she was earning tonight.

I won't let you down, she silently promised her brother.

With her confidence restored, Sienna sprang up from her stool at the spacious dressing table with the intention of exploring her accommodation. It was at least twice the size of her bedsit in London, with a dressing room, a glorious pink marble bathroom full to the brim with expensive products, and a sitting room made comfy with a plump sofa and two easy chairs. And then there was the bed. The size of her bedsit. It took all she'd got not to bounce on it. All in all, this was quite an improvement on her usual changing room at the club. Could she get used to this? You bet, she concluded, turning full circle. It was a shame she wouldn't get the chance.

Having done her research, Sienna had learned quite a bit about the *Acosta Dragon*, but nothing had prepared her for intimate contact with a yacht built to Alejandro's precise specifications. In excess of three hundred feet long, the *Acosta Dragon* was as close to a palace on water as she could imagine. Boasting a nightclub, a cinema, a full gym, several swimming pools, both inside and out, as well as a full spa, there were two helicopters perched like huge black birds on an uppermost deck, as well as a number of small speedboats stored in the hull, for those snap decisions any billionaire might make to spend a day on the beach, she supposed.

Ah, well, enough of that, she concluded as she checked her hair and added a dab of lip gloss. It was time to knock on Jason's door.

'How great is this?' Jason exclaimed the moment he joined her in the corridor.

'I hope my performance lives up to it,' Sienna replied.

'Of course, it will,' Jason assured her. 'Are you sure you're okay?' he added, taking a close look at Sienna.

Musicians were nothing if not speedy at picking up mood.

Alejandro is a musician...

Allegedly. She'd never heard him play. Never seen him play polo, for that matter. She had no idea how he operated in business, apart from market reports saying everything Alejandro Acosta touched turned to gold. Her thighs tingled inconveniently at that thought.

Willing her mind to remain on track as they approached the grand salon, she was only half listening to the officer escorting them, and was wondering what Tom would say if he could see her on Alejandro's superyacht.

Never mind that—what about the fact that her hand was wrapped like a vice around an evening purse containing yet another positive pregnancy test? She'd done one last minute to be absolutely sure, and had taken it with her to show Alejandro at an appropriately discreet moment. Alongside her usual pre-concert nerves, there was another reason for her pulse to race.

CHAPTER EIGHT

SHE WAS AWARE of Alejandro watching her intently throughout her performance. Was he judging her singing, or was it something else causing that disturbingly focused interest?

What was she doing here, anyway? With a world of performers to choose from, why had Alejandro Acosta invited Sienna to sing at his party? It was a strange feeling to sense he wanted her in his bed, yet not to have an inkling of what he was thinking. Being hired as his entertainer tonight made her feel that she was straddling two worlds without a secure foothold in either.

It was a relief to lose herself in music. The atmosphere on board the yacht was very different from the club, but equally warm. One song had led effortlessly into the next, and only one partygoer appeared restless. Alejandro's fierce black gaze had never left her face, and once the applause died down, he came over to speak to her. 'Thank you, Sienna—thank you, Jason.

My guests adored you. You've been everything I expected and more.'

As his brooding look rested on her face, tremors of excitement raced through her body. She had to remind herself that Alejandro was talking about her singing.

'Will you perform again for us tonight?' he asked as a general question to both Jason and Sienna.

'We'd love to,' Jason said.

'If you want me to, of course I will,' Sienna agreed, feeling a glow of pleasure that the evening was going so well.

Would this be a good time to tell him, she wondered as Jason was waylaid by some of the guests. Everywhere she looked there were friendly faces waiting to talk to her too, but she had to take this chance. 'Could we talk in private?' she asked Alejandro.

His brow furrowed, as if he couldn't imagine what she wanted to say. 'It's not about money,' she said quickly.

'What do you want to tell me?' he asked, remaining resolutely in place.

Guests were hovering close by, waiting to talk to Sienna. How could she tell him here? But she had to say something, to remove that suspicious look from his face. 'Do you have a favourite song?'

Alejandro's expression changed enough for her to know that he realised she was swerving his question. 'I'm happy to sing requests,' she added out of sheer desperation.

'Are you changing the subject on purpose? You seem overly anxious to me,' he observed, staring down at her with a frown. 'I'd like to know why.'

'I'm not anxious,' she said too fast. 'What you're seeing is nervous energy.'

Alejandro hummed, as if he didn't believe a word. 'We'll talk later,' he said, making this sound more like a threat than a promise, before moving away to give his guests their chance to meet Sienna.

He had to get away from her or remain at the party with a hard-on. She looked amazing, had sung like an angel, and lied like a demon. What was he to make of that? Apart from the fact that challenge always turned him on, the fact that she was hiding something would plague him for the rest of the night.

Even enjoying the company of his guests couldn't distract him from Sienna. This was another first. How was he supposed to forget how she felt in his arms, or how it felt to make love to her? Was he supposed to concentrate on anything else with Sienna hammering at his mind? To aggravate him all the more, she was currently in conversation with his friend. Sheikh Shahin, the Sheikh of Qabama, was talking animatedly to Sienna. She was listening intently, and occasionally sharing something that amused them both. Were they discussing a song? He doubted that. Shahin was a notorious player. And Sienna appeared to be enjoying the sheikh's company. Was she so easily beguiled, or simply attracted to great wealth?

Was he jealous?

Fortunately, he wasn't required to answer that question, as one of his guests, an elderly senator from the States, stopped by with his very elegant wife to ask Alejandro if Sienna might agree to perform at their anniversary party in Florida.

'I don't speak for Sienna,' he told the senator politely, 'but I'm sure she'd be flattered that you asked.'

'I don't mean to flatter the woman. She's a very talented artiste. We'd send the jet, of course, and she can name her own fee.'

Sienna as paid entertainer didn't sit well with him, and the senator's question had forced him to ask himself what he was doing tonight but paying Sienna for her services. Biting back impatience at his own crass lack of judgement, he promised the senator that he'd pass on his message—just as soon as Sienna finished chatting to the sheikh.

He was glad of a reason to do so. His main concern was that Sienna had some sort of plan going forward. The last ten minutes had brought home to him the fact that she could so easily end up flitting around the world, singing for people like him and the senator, but would she make enough to sustain her career? Having promised Tom that he'd take care of Sienna, that was exactly what he intended to do.

Interrupting her conversation with Shahin, he drew her aside. 'You were stunning tonight. Thank you again.'

'But?' she said, flashing a glance at his friend the sheikh, who'd had enough good sense to step back, but who was now watching them with his dark, hawkish stare.

'I worry about you,' he said as he steered her away. 'You're a beautiful woman, and a talented singer, and I'm concerned that you don't have a plan in place to see you go on to greater success after tonight.'

'As a matter of fact, I do,' she said. 'I'm planning to do what I love. I'm going to teach. I can't think of anything better than sharing the happiness I feel when I'm wrapped up in music, and with as many people as I can.'

'That is a good plan,' he agreed, 'and I'd like to hear more.'

'Can we talk now?' she asked with a degree of urgency that surprised him.

In the middle of his party? But now he noticed that Sienna's hand had tightened around her evening purse, turning her knuckles white. What was so vital that she had to tell him now? Glancing around, he concluded that his guests, still high on their enjoyment of Sienna's performance, were unlikely to miss them. Ushering her inside, he took her to his suite. 'Tell me what's worrying you,' he said as he closed the door. 'Sienna?' he pressed as her eyes filled with tears.

'I don't know how to tell you this…'

'Just make a start,' he encouraged, and, because it felt right in that moment, he brought her into his arms.

'I don't want to make it all about me,' she blurted, staring up with wounded eyes.

Why shouldn't it be about Sienna for once? He hated seeing her like this. Drawing her close, he cupped the back of her head to kiss her, tenderly at first, and then with increasing passion.

Erotic fever blanked her mind. The moment to tell Alejandro about their child vanished in a frantic need to be one with him. Knowing they had to get back to the party only added urgency to their actions. There was no time for finesse. Turning her against the wall, he cupped her buttocks with one hand and freed himself with the other. Urging him on, she exhaled noisily with relief as he tossed her thong aside and plunged deep. She bucked greedily against him, with only one thought in mind, and it was only seconds later that she screamed out her release.

'More,' she gasped as he planted one fist against the wall above her head. Supporting her with his other hand, Alejandro began to move deeply, rhythmically, rotating his hips to add to her pleasure. The outcome was as swift as it was inevitable. Was his suite soundproof? She could only hope.

'Relax,' he said with a smile in his voice as he caressed her back with long, even strokes. 'Just concentrate on what I'm doing to you and let me do the rest.'

With pleasure. With immense pleasure—

Not taking this chance to tell Alejandro about their baby was foolish, but she couldn't think while he was plunging her into pleasure again.

He cared for this woman. The realisation swamped him as Sienna collapsed, sated, in his arms. He'd never known a woman like her. There'd been a desperation to her lovemaking that left her vulnerable, and yet she was so strong. The contrast perplexed him. She was self-willed, he reflected as he watched her drift off to a level of consciousness that was only just above sleep. She had wanted to tell him something, but there wasn't time now.

Carrying her into his bedroom, he laid her down carefully on the bed. There was no reason why she had to rush back to the party. She'd given her all when she sang to his guests. It was time for her to sleep now.

A fast shower later, and he was dressed, ready to return to the party. Pausing at the door, he glanced across his bedroom at Sienna. Deeply asleep, she looked so calm and contented. There was no reason to disturb her. Whatever she had wanted to tell him could wait.

He was about to leave the room when he noticed her evening purse had fallen onto the floor, strewing its contents across the carpet. Returning, he hunkered down to retrieve it, doing the best he could to stuff everything safely back inside. He was about to put the purse on the nightstand, where she'd see it as soon as she woke, when he realised what he was looking at. Cursing softly, he examined the pregnancy test sticking out of the top. The torch on his cell revealed two distinct blue lines.

Sienna was pregnant?

With his child?

Of course, with his child. Everything made sense now. She was expecting his child. Far from feeling nothing, he was finding it a struggle to balance control and his undeniable emotional reaction to the fact that they were expecting a child.

Why hadn't she told him? Didn't she trust him? He glanced down at Sienna. Was he to blame for her lack of trust? Realising that she was probably frightened to tell him, because he'd always been so emotionally restrained, cut through him like a knife. But any discussion would have to wait. His guests had been neglected long enough. The party was due to end soon. He had to be on hand to thank everyone for accepting his invitation. After which, he would instruct the captain to prepare for immediate departure.

With Sienna still on board?

Fear of losing those he loved was nothing compared to the thought of losing touch with his unborn child. By the time Sienna woke, they'd be at sea. No longer was she simply Tom's sister, or the woman Tom had left half an island to, Sienna was the mother of his child. *His* daughter or son.

Their child.

He frowned at the thought of a new life connecting them for ever, uncertain as to how he felt about that. There was a lot he would have to get used to, he accepted as a discreet tap sounded on the door.

His purser was waiting to speak to him.

'The ambassador and his wife are about to leave, sir. I thought you would want to know.'

'Thank you. Yes. I'm coming now.' With one final glance at Sienna, he left her to sleep.

CHAPTER NINE

WAKING TO MEMORIES of being naked in Alejandro's arms, Sienna concluded that she'd had the best sleep ever. But now she must hurry to get back to the party. Alejandro had already left, she realised as she traced the indentation left by his powerful body on the crisp white sheets. Remembering everything, she stretched her limbs with a sigh of contentment. Swinging out of bed on a wave of optimism, she felt confident that it would be easy now to tell him about their baby.

Sex brings people closer…

It must go some way to doing that, she mused as doubt set in.

How would Alejandro handle her news? With a bank draft, or with his heart?

If he felt the same way she did, there was nothing to worry about, she determined as she felt her way around the stateroom. It was pitch black inside Alejandro's bedroom, and she wasn't sure where the light was. The torch on her phone lit the way—and then she saw her evening purse open on the nightstand, with the positive pregnancy test sticking out of the top.

Panic ripped through her at the thought that Alejandro knew she was pregnant. What must he think about her leaving him to find out, rather than telling him straight? As soon as she'd discovered the test was positive, he should have been the first to know.

Calm down. It's not too late.

If her hectic pulse would only slow down, she would go to find him, and explain.

Rushing into the bathroom, she took the fastest shower ever, and barely dried herself, before shoehorning her still-damp body back into her gown. Squeezing her feet into shoes that suddenly seemed several sizes too small, she steadied herself against the wall—

She steadied herself...

The River Thames was tidal, but—

Rushing across the room, she dragged back the drapes. The meagre sunlight of early morning sifted through the clouds, revealing a ragged ocean, and not much else besides.

'Jason!' Frantic to find him, she exploded out of the room. Hammering on Jason's door, she yelled at the top of her voice, 'Jason! Are you there?'

'Can I help you, ma'am?'

Only now did she refocus to see the uniformed steward standing patiently by. Composing herself, she battled to keep her voice steady enough to ask, 'I'm looking for my friend Mr Mullings? The pianist who accompanied me last night?'

With a smile, the steward relaxed. 'What a wonderful musician he is—'

'Have you seen him?' Politeness was lost in the panic of the moment.

'Yes, ma'am,' the steward confirmed, obviously concerned now he realised how upset she was. 'Mr Mullings left the yacht with the rest of the guests, shortly before we sailed last night—'

'We sailed? Last night?' Her voice had turned mouse small. How could Alejandro allow his yacht to sail without warning her first?

Why wouldn't he, when he knew she was pregnant? His shock must have been at least equal to hers.

'Mr Mullings asked me to tell you how much he'd enjoyed the evening, and that he hoped to see you very soon.'

Very soon? That was a vain hope, Sienna suspected. Her brain began to whirl as she struggled to find answers. Jason must have known she was still onboard. Why hadn't he warned her what was happening? She had to speak to him right away—

Jason would hardly call by Alejandro's stateroom to find out what was going on. And wasn't it more important to confront Alejandro right now? Yes, she should have told him that she was pregnant, but that didn't give Alejandro the right to keep her onboard while the *Acosta Dragon* sailed out of London.

Realising that the steward was still waiting patiently, she took a deep, steadying breath before asking, 'Could you please tell me where to find Señor Acosta?'

'He's in the breakfast room, *señorita*. Would you like to join him? Or I could arrange for food to be sent to your room?'

And seem afraid to show her face? 'I don't want to put you to any extra trouble, so if it's all right with you, I'd prefer to join Señor Acosta.'

'Of course. As soon as you're ready, just call me.'

The steward kept his eyeline commendably high, sparing Sienna the embarrassment of wearing last night's clothes. 'That's very kind of you,' she said, adding with a tight smile, 'Also, would you happen to have a phone charger?'

'Certainly, ma'am.'

Going back inside the stateroom, she shut the door and leaned against it. There was no point panicking. She was stranded at sea with a billionaire who'd just learned he was the father of her child. She'd handle it, as she handled everything else, with calm reason. Fairly calmly—maybe not calmly at all, she accepted as a knock sounded on the door.

'Your phone charger, ma'am.'

She breathed a sigh of relief. 'Thank you so much.' At least she now had the means to contact the outside world.

'Kidnapped?' Alejandro barely glanced up from his phone when she confronted him in the dining room. 'Don't you think that's overly dramatic?'

His gaze pierced her. Okay, guilty as charged, but she was going to become a mother, and that required strength and resolve. 'What would you call leaving London without informing the only remaining guest on board that the *Acosta Dragon* was sailing?'

'Hospitality?'

She wasn't fooled by Alejandro's relaxed manner. That wasn't a joke. Tension radiated from him in suffocating waves. 'Just tell me why you've done this, Alejandro.'

'I would have thought that was obvious.' Lifting his head, he studied her without warmth. 'Why did you hide the fact that you're pregnant?'

'I didn't hide it—'

'You just didn't get around to telling me?'

The chilling timbre of his voice made it sound as if they were two strangers who had never shared a moment's intimacy, and all that had ever been between them was sex.

'I only just found out myself.'

'And there hasn't been a single chance to tell me?' he suggested with a sceptical stare.

'I can only tell you the truth, Alejandro. I would never leave you out of such an important fact on purpose.'

'No,' he drawled. 'So, instead you decide to spend one more night in my bed.'

'That's not how it was!' she shot back. 'You make it sound so—'

'Tawdry?' he supplied.

'No! How can you even think that?'

'I'm supposed to believe you forgot that you were carrying my child?'

A desperate, sinking feeling told Sienna there was no coming back from this. Alejandro had retreated into his old, cold ways, but she would not be blamed for something they had both wanted, and told him straight. 'I forgot everything last night. You did too.'

With a shake of his head, he dismissed her, but the *Acosta Dragon* had other ideas, and chose that moment to lurch. Staggering, she flailed around for something to cling onto. Alejandro was on his feet in an instant. Taking firm hold of her, he guided her to a chair. 'Sit down before you fall down,' he commanded, but concern had returned to his voice.

'I was going to tell you last night,' she explained, seeking his gaze and holding it.

'But you didn't,' he said.

Sensing once again that he was withdrawing emotionally, she refused to let him stay in that ivory tower. 'I didn't tell you because we were making love,' she insisted. 'Or, at least, I was.'

'You trusted me with your body, to the point that you were happy to fall asleep in my arms, but you couldn't trust me enough to tell me about our child,' Alejandro said with a disbelieving shake of his head.

They had briefly shared something special, and she had trusted Alejandro absolutely, but that only made his cynical reading of the situation harder to take. 'If you'd only woken me before we sailed—'

'You would have told me then?' he queried in a cold tone.

Something inside her snapped. 'What's wrong with you, Alejandro? Are you frightened you might come to care too much for a child?'

'Frightened of releasing my emotions, as you are?' he suggested bitterly.

'I didn't have much trouble last night,' she fired back in full warrior mode.

Turning his back on her, he began to pace the room, but she refused to leave it there.

'Is this attack your way of avoiding how you'll feel when you hold our child in your arms?'

Stopping dead, he wheeled around. 'The consequence of bringing another innocent life into the world has always been glaringly apparent to me.'

'But not to me?' she suggested. 'Why are we attacking each other, Alejandro? Shouldn't we be rejoicing? I'll make no excuse for being pregnant. If you must know, I'm glad. I didn't even realise how much I wanted this baby until I remembered the relationship I was lucky enough to have with my own mother. It was then I realised that I had a chance to recreate all those precious moments with my own child. The moment I saw those two blue lines, I was in love, and I can't wait for our baby to be born. Whether that's convenient for you, or not,' she added, with a direct but compassionate stare into Alejandro's hooded eyes.

Reaching out, she touched his arm, but Alejandro had gone beyond her reach, and he felt stiff and unyielding. If only she could read that inscrutable mind. She guessed that he was hurt that she'd excluded him, even for a short time, but she couldn't repair that now, and it was vital they both moved forward. 'Alejandro...' She spoke softly, gently. 'I'm so sorry I didn't tell you right away.'

'Where are you going?' he asked as she got up to leave the breakfast table. Standing, he barred her way. 'It isn't safe for you to go anywhere, until the wind drops—'

The words had barely left his mouth when the deck bucked again. And again, he saved her. Being safe in Alejandro's arms felt better than anything else on earth, and tears began to spill down her cheeks. If only things had been different, less complicated, they should have been celebrating this news, rather than confronting each other.

Allowing him to steer her back to a chair, she sat down and admitted, 'I wanted the news to be as special for you, as it has been for me. As soon as I knew, everything changed—my horizons, my hopes and dreams. Don't worry,' she added with a faint smile. 'I'm not about to ask you for anything. I can handle this by myself.'

'I don't understand,' Alejandro protested. 'You're speaking as if you're on your own. Is it your intention to cut me out?'

'I would never do that. I'm trying to reassure you that I don't plan to be a—'

'A drag on me?' Alejandro suggested. 'What are you imagining, Sienna? Do you seriously think I'd wash my hands of a woman who is carrying my child? What sort of man do you take me for?'

'I don't really know,' she admitted. As long as she'd known him, which, admittedly, wasn't long, Alejandro had steered clear of emotional involvement, and she wasn't much better. Craving the closeness of the family she'd lost had left Sienna believing that she'd never find that certainty again. Getting close to anyone was scary. The closer you got, the more you stood to lose. Desperation filled her. How could the two of them, with all their hang-ups, hope to successfully raise a child?

Pregnancy hormones had a lot to answer for, Sienna told herself sensibly. Closing her eyes, she settled her thoughts. Her first thought was for Tom, and why he'd put her in the way of this man, only to drive them apart. 'It would have been better if we'd never met,' she mused out loud on the heels of this thought.

'But we have met,' Alejandro pointed out bluntly, 'And now you're expecting my child.'

Trying to imagine such a formidable man playing father to his children, and giving them the great life Sienna's father had made sure she'd had, proved a hard ask. Protecting her stomach with one hand, she voiced her innermost fears. 'This baby isn't *your* child, Alejandro, it's *ours*.'

'If you think for one moment that I don't take

responsibility seriously,' he replied in a voice of menacing quiet, 'you'll find out how wrong you are. When it comes to my brothers' and sister's children, I would do anything for them.'

The fire in his eyes, and the resolve in the set of his chin, said everything about money, control, and power. What chance did she have against that?

Every chance. She was a mother.

'Sharing a child is nothing like sharing an island,' she said, firming her jaw.

'You think I don't know that?'

Now she saw that his face was strained as he spoke, and compassion rose inside her as Alejandro continued, 'I will play a full part in the raising of my child. Anything less would be an insult to my father, who was the most wonderful man. I won't deny my child the same chance to know me.'

Of everything he'd said, she found this the most poignant. Locked away in his tightly controlled world, Alejandro didn't realise how isolated he'd made himself, and as she spoke her heart reached out to his. 'You can see our baby at any time—'

'Obviously.'

His expression chilled her even more as he continued, 'I doubt you could stop me.'

'Why would I want to stop you?'

'Will the visits be at a time to suit you?' he fired back.

Alejandro was referring to the reading of Tom's will, where everything had been done to suit him. 'I wouldn't be so inconsiderate. Any arrangement I make must suit both of us.'

'Don't worry,' Alejandro told her with a long, assessing look. 'I will make sure that they do.'

Did that mean he intended to keep her close until their baby was born, when she would become superfluous to requirements and dismissed? Alejandro could easily afford an army of nannies. With the power he wielded, Alejandro Acosta could do anything he damn well liked. All of this overwhelmed her, and it took a moment to grind her brain into gear again. 'I'd like to disembark at the next port,' she said once she'd got her thoughts straight. 'I'll return home, make a plan, see a doctor—'

'The next port is the island,' Alejandro said, cutting her off.

'*The* island?' It was a surprise to feel how excited she was, at finally arriving at a place that had meant so much to Tom.

'That's right,' Alejandro confirmed. 'I was heading back, and thought this would be the ideal opportunity for you to view your inheritance.'

She'd inherited a lot more than an island,

judging by that suspicion in Alejandro's eyes. Did he really think she was a gold-digger, only interested in what Tom had left in the monetary sense? That hurt. After everything they'd been to each other, everything she'd thought they'd meant to each other, while she was confiding in Alejandro, how could he think such a thing?

And now the doubts really set in. When she'd boarded his yacht, she'd got the sense of leaving her world behind and entering his. How much more would that apply when they landed on an island that was as good as Alejandro's private fiefdom, from where there might be no escape? 'I really need to make some calls before we reach the island,' she said as her panic rose.

'Of course,' Alejandro said calmly.

Was she guilty of overreacting? It was impossible to tell from his face. Finding yourself at sea on a billionaire's yacht tended to muddle a brain, she concluded, and all that really mattered was putting the interests of their baby first.

'We're both angry,' she said in an attempt to smooth things over. 'And that's not good for our baby. I'd like to start over.'

Alejandro was not so easily persuaded. 'Start over?' he asked, staring at her from beneath a lowered brow. 'Would that be from before or after you joined me in bed?'

'For the first or second time?' she shot back.

Like two combatants in a ring, facing each other unblinking, neither of them was prepared to look away first. It was a relief when Alejandro broke the silence, but he did so with the most surprising question yet. 'Have you eaten since yesterday?'

'Some nibbles at the party,' she said, thinking back.

'And do you think that's sensible, for a pregnant woman?'

'Do you intend to monitor my behaviour throughout this pregnancy?'

'Someone should.'

They were in danger of returning to the silent stand-off, and once again Alejandro spoke first. 'There is a difference between control and caring.'

And nothing to be gained by remaining stubborn, Sienna accepted, though she could have used a handy manual to teach her how to deal with a billionaire she barely knew, whose child she was expecting.

'Choose something and eat,' Alejandro encouraged.

As he lifted up a basket of flaky treats, Sienna was reminded that she was ravenous. 'Good,' he said as she began to eat. 'I'm sure you feel better now.'

She almost laughed, he sounded so much like Tom. Both Alejandro and Tom had been forced to take on the role of both parents. Tom's care and concern had sometimes felt smothering. Now she realised that love had driven her brother's actions, and that Alejandro must have done the same for his siblings. Similarities between the two men had never occurred to her before. Alejandro was accustomed to taking responsibility for his family, and would find it hard to relinquish that role. Understanding this made it easier to open up. 'I need something from you.'

'Butter? Or jam?'

Pressing her lips together, to avoid laughing out loud, she said, 'Clothes? I can't wear this gown the entire time. And I need to call Jason.' She frowned as she remembered. 'People need to know where I am.'

'And the manager of your club,' Alejandro reminded her. 'He'll be concerned about your safety too. You'll have to tell him that you won't be coming in for a while. Relax. Eat. We'll sort everything out later.'

They'd sort everything out now, Sienna determined. 'You have helicopters on board, don't you? Why can't I fly back to London?'

'In this weather?'

Her heart sank as she followed Alejandro's gaze outside the window, to where rain mercilessly lashed the deck. Quickly recalculating, she said, 'So, Tom's island is our next port of call?'

'Correct,' Alejandro confirmed. 'The island you now own half of.'

The warmth that had flared briefly between them was instantly gone. It was obvious to Sienna that Alejandro was still furious at the way Tom had written his will. But the fact remained that the half she owned was Sienna's to do with as she wished. If only Alejandro could see that she would never ride roughshod over anyone. Of course, she'd consult with him first. She'd always keep him in the loop. Would *he* agree to her raising their child?

Her hand flew instinctively to her stomach, where their baby, in its innocence, was growing stronger every day, vulnerable to the decisions they made.

CHAPTER TEN

He was going to be a father.

NOTHING ELSE MATTERED. Staring out over the starboard rail, he realised how much he loved wild, elemental weather. It suited his nature, he supposed. He loved anything with a challenge attached—except for one, infuriating woman. 'Sienna!' He whirled around. 'What are you doing out here? Can't you see how dangerous it is?'

'But safe for you?' she suggested.

He wasn't a pregnant woman. Taking hold of her, he steadied her, to keep her safe.

She felt so warm and soft in his arms. It would be easy to forget how strong Sienna was. 'This weather is dangerous.'

'And you're not?' she said with a lift of her chin. 'Lucky you don't frighten me.'

'Evidently,' he agreed.

Guiding her back inside, he took her to his

study. 'Can we talk now?' she asked as he closed the door.

'Of course.'

'What were you thinking out there?'

'How to kidnap my next victim,' he suggested, tongue in cheek.

She almost smiled, and then said, 'Truce?'

'Coming from you, I take that as a compliment.'

'Don't,' she warned, turning serious. 'I'm only suggesting a truce between us because, very soon, there will be a very important addition to you and me.'

'For once, I agree with you,' he confirmed, surprising himself by how relieved he was that they were talking again. Life without Sienna was something he was finding increasingly hard to imagine. Everything he'd once thought important had been relegated to a distant second place. Nothing mattered more to him than the welfare of mother and baby. It was because of that that he'd keep her close, as his father had cared for his mother throughout all her pregnancies. Except, unlike his own mother, Sienna would never have to work another day in her life if she didn't want to. Remembering this, he smiled. Sienna would be right up there with the best of mothers. Her warmth, strength and resilience would make sure of that. She'd be the bedrock of any family.

His family?

He shifted in his seat. Love was the final taboo. Like a distant promise he didn't deserve, it was a reality for so many, but not for him. Until he could forgive himself for allowing his parents to take that flight, he could never rejoice about anything fully, because that only brought on crushing guilt. Destined to go through life wondering, if he'd called his parents, could he have stopped them taking that flight had left him incapable of relaxing his hold on anything it was possible to control. Only by concentrating on the practical could he blank out the emotion.

'Alejandro?' Sienna prompted with concern. 'You okay?'

'Yes,' he said in a distracted monotone.

'Come and look,' she said, grabbing his hand briefly in her excitement to look out of the window. 'I can't believe this. The rain has stopped, the wind has dropped, and the sea is as flat as a pancake.'

'That's the magic pull of the island.' In spite of his doubts about Sienna, she'd been through a lot, and he couldn't deny that it felt good to see her smile.

'Is that grey smudge on the horizon the island?' she asked in a voice tense with pent-up excitement.

'Yes, it is,' he confirmed.

He allowed himself an indulgent moment, during which he imagined raising a child on the island. It was the perfect place to bring up children, and Sienna's news had supercharged his plans. When his child was old enough, they could ski together in the morning, and bathe in the warm surf during late afternoon. That happy combination was just one of the reasons that had led him and Tom to the same conclusion, that there was nowhere better to build a rehabilitation centre for injured vets. Nothing could be allowed to stand in the way of that.

'Is it safe to go up on deck now?'

He turned to look at Sienna. 'Of course—' She was already heading for the door. That was the magic of the island. There was still so much to talk about: the island, their baby, the future, but as land grew slowly closer and more distinct, and their destination revealed itself in all its summer glory, he knew that questions could wait, because they would unfold organically on-shore, without the past or preconceived ideas getting in the way.

He found her leaning over the rail. 'I can't wait to explore,' she enthused.

He couldn't remain immune to Sienna's enthusiasm, which was only increased by the crowd on the dock, waiting to greet them. 'Look at this, Alejandro! *Look at this!*'

His fellow islanders were naturally curious to see Sienna. Tom's sister was a draw in herself, because Tom had been a huge favourite on the island. Today, she would stand at his side, and, very soon, their child would join him.

'I can't believe how many people have come to see you,' she exclaimed as she waved to the crowd. 'I had no idea how friendly the people here would be, or how incredibly beautiful this island could be.'

Seeing the land through Sienna's eyes was a revelation. The dock was neat and clean, and everything looked prosperous. The road beyond the dock was well maintained, like all the roads on the island, but it was the spectacular country-side that really captured his attention. Framed by it, Sienna had never looked more beautiful to him.

'Tom never got the chance to show me any photographs,' she explained with a wistful note in her voice. 'I had no idea he owned something like this.'

'Half of this,' he felt it only fair to remind her.

Troubled questions clouded her eyes when she turned to look at him. 'Of course,' she said softly. 'I hadn't forgotten.'

He hadn't mentioned buying back Sienna's half of the island for some time now, which had maybe given her the wrong idea—that he'd given up. This was not the case. Her idea to lease any part of the island she didn't use back to him wouldn't fly, so he'd ignored the suggestion. Parcelling up this land into even smaller plots would be an insult to the islanders, and he would never agree to anything that might upset them.

He watched as ropes were tossed to shore, and raised a hand to acknowledge the cheers from countless voices. 'It will be my pleasure to show you around,' he told Sienna. She had to see, in order to understand.

'What will everyone think when I disembark in my evening dress?' she asked with sudden concern.

'That's not going to happen. See over there...' He pointed to where a team of men were carrying a number of suitcases on board.

'I don't understand. What's happening?' Sienna asked.

'I've arranged—or rather, my PA has arranged—for clothes to be delivered this morning for you.'

'Now I've seen everything,' Sienna admitted, standing back with a sigh. 'Is there anything your magic wand can't conjure up?'

He shrugged. 'Not much.'

'Well, thank you for thinking about me. And don't worry, I'll pay you back for anything I choose.'

'There's no need,' he said, not wanting to talk about money. He didn't want anything to spoil their arrival on the island. 'Why don't you go and choose something to wear?'

'There's every need to talk about money,' Sienna insisted.

'Later, then,' he agreed as she hurried off.

It was good to see Sienna return in a casual outfit of jeans and a loose blouse. Good? She looked hot. Distraction was needed fast. 'If there's anything else you need, my housekeeper, Maria, will be glad to source it for you. Practically anything can be couriered over to the ranch house, and Maria is a dab hand with alterations, or she could even run up a dress for you herself.'

'You are a very lucky man,' Sienna observed, frowning a little at his burst of information.

'I'm extremely lucky to have Maria care for my home,' he agreed as they made their way through the crowd. This took some considerable time, as Sienna, who was warmly received, was making it her business to chat with everyone she could. He did too. It was a great start, and they were both reluctant to leave when he finally led the way to an open-topped Jeep. 'In her youth, Maria was a seamstress for a top Spanish couturier,' he explained as he opened the door for Sienna.

'This is the most you've ever told me about anything,' she said as he climbed in beside her. 'I'm in real danger of getting to know you.'

'Impossible,' he returned dryly.

'Well, I can't wait to meet Maria, but please tell Maria that I don't need any fuss.'

He laughed to himself. That wouldn't work. Maria's life was all about caring for others. 'I will,' he promised, keeping those doubts to himself.

Alejandro had taken time to speak to everyone on the dock, and he'd introduced her around, Sienna remembered. Their warm reception had been such a thrill. And now this beautiful island. She could almost forget that Alejandro had brought her here in the most unconventional way, because this was the perfect place to launch the Tom Slater trust.

'I used to come here on holiday with my parents,' he revealed as they drove through sun-kissed vistas of rolling green hills and blue, blue skies.

She stared at him with interest. 'And then you bought the island.'

'It seemed a fitting memorial.'

After he said this, Alejandro's face closed down, as if he'd said too much. Remembering the past would always be painful, until he built on the loving memories he shared with his parents, instead of blaming himself for the fact they were no longer here.

To reinforce this thought, he gunned the engine and they took off at speed. She refused to be nervous. Responsibility meant everything to Alejandro, and he had the mother of his baby sitting next to him. He wouldn't take any chances.

'How could you not fall in love with this island?' she exclaimed as they reached the summit of a hill to find the calm azure ocean spread out in front of them. 'Paradise doesn't even come close.'

I understand you better now, Tom. No wonder you loved this special place and wanted me to discover it for myself. I only have one regret, and that is that we can't explore together—

'Do you like what you see?'

Alejandro distracted her. 'I certainly do,' she said with feeling. And it wasn't just the island she admired, but Alejandro. There was such strength in him, and as they drove on she noticed he was becoming more relaxed. She'd never seen him like this before, and it warmed her to see him happy here.

Settling back in her seat, she enjoyed the rest of the drive. Tom's dream had been to build a home on the island and settle down, and now it was as if Tom had passed that dream on. The more she saw of the magical island, the calmer she felt. This was the place where Tom's dream would become a reality.

Alejandro's sprawling ranch house was beyond impressive. She might have known. Of all his dwellings, this was the one that spoke to her the most, maybe because it was rustic, rather than grand, but she could see the care in every inch of the sprawling wooden structure. The grounds surrounding it were immaculately groomed, and it stood at the end of a very long drive. There were no gates to that drive, none needed for a man who owned the island.

Half an island, she amended with the same spear of surprise that always hit her when she realised that the other half belonged to her.

Alejandro had brought the Jeep to a halt in front of a large, arched front door, in front of which an older woman stood waiting to greet them.

'My housekeeper, Maria,' Alejandro explained. Sienna was immediately drawn to the warmth on Maria's face. His housekeeper couldn't have appeared more welcoming if she'd tried. The moment Sienna was out of the Jeep, she advanced, arms opened wide. 'Welcome—come in. We've been so excited since we knew you were coming. Tom's sister,' Maria exclaimed, studying Sienna's face with shrewd, raisin-black eyes. 'Yes. I can see your brother in you.' She smiled. 'And you in him,' she added warmly. 'I hope your journey has been smooth?'

Fortunately, Sienna didn't get chance to answer. What was the point in telling this lovely woman that her boss was an unscrupulous rogue who stopped at nothing to get his own way? As she worked for him, Maria probably knew that already, Sienna reasoned as she revealed, 'We did have some choppy water…' She stared pointedly at Alejandro. 'But as soon as we arrived here, the sun began to shine again.'

'Perfect,' Maria remarked as she led Sienna into the house.

'It's wonderful to be in a place that meant so much to my brother,' Sienna said quietly as they stood in the hall.

Taking both Sienna's hands in hers, Maria told her, 'We're so very glad to see you.'

'As I am to be here.'

'Before I take you to your room, there's something I'd like to ask you.'

'Yes?'

'I'm sorry to throw this at you the minute you arrive, but we always have a fiesta when Señor Acosta comes home, and this time I wondered if we could dedicate the celebration to your brother?'

'I'd love that, and I know Tom would too.' As Alejandro was right behind them, she felt it only right to check with him.

'If it makes you happy...?'

'It does.' It would make her happier still to put a smile on Alejandro's face. Coming back to the island had made him briefly glad, and had obviously made him relax. Now, she suspected that thoughts about a party for Tom had plunged him back into the past. She looked from him to Maria. Were they keeping something from her? Something about Tom they thought might upset her, perhaps?

'If it's all right with you, Alejandro,' she said carefully, 'I think that's a lovely idea. Tom loved a party.' For some reason, she found herself thinking back to how wild Tom could become at a celebration. 'He wouldn't have wanted any of us to be sad,' she said with more determination.

Another glance at Alejandro was enough to tell her that the shutters were well and truly down. 'I'm sure Tom will be cheering us on,' she said to reassure Maria, who, Sienna now noticed, was also staring with concern at her boss.

Maria turned out to be a dab hand at diplomacy. 'With your permission, *señorita*—and, of course, with Señor Acosta's permission...' Alejandro gave a curt nod. 'That is what we shall do,' Maria decreed. 'And I will arrange everything for you.'

'Thank you, Maria.' She gave the older woman a hug. With people like Maria around, Sienna's plans for her share of the island didn't seem quite so out of reach.

And Alejandro? What will he have to say about your plans?

She would have to hope that a deeper understanding grew between them. Give it time.

An understanding? Is that enough for you?

It would have to be, Sienna concluded as she followed Maria deeper into the house.

It was impossible to remain under the same roof as Sienna without lust plaguing him. And he wanted to show her the island. He wanted so much, too much. Leaving her in Maria's capable hands, he left the house to drive about a mile or so; anywhere to give him distance. Halting the vehicle beside one of the vast paddocks, he climbed out to whistle up one of his ponies. Riding bareback, he headed out at the gallop without any clear destination in mind. Just not back to the ranch was currently enough for him.

So much had happened between him and Sienna, he needed mind space to think. How much did she know about Tom? Did she know that when the darkness came, Tom could be violent and unpredictable? That same darkness had claimed Tom on the night he was killed. Having defied Alejandro's orders, Tom had placed their entire group in danger, and had paid the ultimate price. Should he tell Sienna that?

As soon as he reached the long, flat shoreline, he urged his horse into the surf. Pounding through the waves was exhilarating. His earliest memories had been forged here. Happy family events, too numerous to count, so when the island had come up for sale, it had seemed obvious to seize the opportunity to make more memories. But he would not forget the past. Reining in, he stared out to sea, recalling his belief that men like Tom could be healed if they were this close to nature. It hadn't taken him long to persuade Tom to believe it too, and a project they could both work on had come out of that. He had hoped Tom would be one of the first to be cured here.

Alejandro Acosta, known in the forces as the Master of Control, had never been able to explain his close friendship with Wild Tom, as others in their platoon had called Tom. He didn't need to explain their friendship. They were firm friends, and that had always been enough. Occasionally, Alejandro saw the same wildness in himself, and they had definitely shared a vision. Care for all living creatures, and a deep appreciation of the natural world, added to the fact that Tom could always make him laugh, which was a small thing, but a rare and beautiful thing.

Turning his horse, he allowed it to amble along the lacy fringes of the surf. Tom had been a dreamer, not a doer, hence the broken-down ranch house Sienna had inherited. She was cut from a very different cloth from her brother. Determination could have been her middle name. He could imagine her, spade in her hand, digging the foundations herself, and probably singing an aria as she did so.

Smiling as he thought about Sienna, he realised he was growing dangerously fond of her. She lightened him, as Tom had, and lifted him, but could he commit fully, knowing how he'd pulled back in the past? And would she want that, or were all her thoughts for the island and Tom?

It was late afternoon by the time he arrived back at the house. He walked in at the very moment Sienna came downstairs. The luminosity of her beauty hit him like a punch in the gut.

Memories of how abandoned she'd been in his arms, in his bed, instantly flooded his mind, but Sienna had on a businesslike expression, and lost no time in telling him what her future plans involved.

'Alejandro, we need to talk.'

'No problem. I'll get cleaned up, then we'll meet in my study downstairs, okay?'

Her wildflower scent assailed him as he jogged up the stairs. Thanks to his PA, Sienna had a whole world of designer clothes to choose from, but had picked out fresh jeans and a simple white top. No make-up, and with her hair drawn back, she looked effortlessly beautiful, beautifully understated. And keen to talk.

He found her in the kitchen, chatting to Maria, and suggested they go to his orangery, which was one of his favourite rooms in the house. The huge glass structure overlooked his ponies, grazing contentedly in the paddocks beyond. The ambience was restful, and he thought it perfect for their talks. Simply decorated, with plants and rugs and ethnic throws, this was his choice, rather than an interior designer's. He always found it a toss-up between staring out at the mesmerising view or simply contemplating the interior of a most attractive space.

'You have a beautiful home,' Sienna observed. 'Each time I think I've seen perfection, I discover more here, and it tells me a lot about you.'

'I think you'd better explain that,' he said.

'My guess is this is all you.'

He laughed. 'You found me out.' He was glad that it pleased her.

'It isn't dreary,' she said thoughtfully.

He laughed again and held up his hand. 'I'd stop there, if I were you. I built this house with the help of my friends on the island. Something else bothering you?' he asked as she frowned.

'Two things,' she admitted.

'Start with the first,' he advised, settling back.

'Okay.' She launched straight in. 'I'm going to build a music facility here on my part of the island. I dreamed of doing something like this for years, and now I can. I'm planning to build a music therapy centre, to be exact.'

'That's the first thing. What's the second?'

'Sounds silly after that, but the clothes your PA sent are a bit confusing. Do you expect me to sing while I'm here?'

'No,' he said with surprise. 'Why?'

'Just that evening clothes don't seem appropriate wear for a ranch?'

'Perhaps my PA imagined I might fly you to the Ritz for a meal.'

Sienna hummed. 'Do you do that often?'

'Why? Are you jealous?'

'No,' she protested, rather too fast and too loud.

'I don't expect you to do anything while you're here, but take a view of your land,' he said.

'Do the deal and leave?' she suggested.

'I didn't say that.'

'So, what do you think of my plan?'

'I'm reserving judgement for now. On the face of it, it sounds interesting.'

'You could sound more enthusiastic.'

'You want the truth—you'll soon be having my child, and I don't understand how you're going to handle becoming a first-time mother while you run such an important institution.'

'First off, I doubt it will be built in a few months.'

'But you might need to rest during your pregnancy, and then what?'

'There's a third question.'

'Go on,' he invited.

'Why are there so many business suits amongst those new clothes, when I've never owned a suit in my life?'

'I thought you'd be more comfortable if you were formally dressed for any meetings with lawyers.'

'Lawyers?' Sienna sounded shocked. 'Should I appoint someone?'

'I can advise—'

'Thank you,' she interrupted. 'I'm sure you can, but legal advice is something I prefer to handle myself.'

'As you wish.'

I do wish, her glance told him. He put his hands up, palms flat. 'This doesn't need to become a confrontation. I only meant to suggest that when we firm things up for the transfer of the land from Tom's name to yours, you should have independent legal advice.'

'Oh.' She seemed lost for a moment. 'I just thought with us being as close as two people can be, and the fact that we've confided in each other, and discussed so many things, you have previously seemed evasive when it comes to the land or our baby.'

'Is that what you think? I don't.'

'Okay, so maybe we're both guilty of not explaining our feelings clearly. Can you even remember the last time you admitted how you felt about anything?'

'Can you?' he asked.

They were both haunted by the past, but must not allow that to impact the future of an innocent child. They sat in silence for a while, until

Sienna prompted, 'So, where does that leave us, Alejandro?'

'More than two people thrown together because of Tom, I hope,' he admitted.

He could tell she was surprised by his candour, and her next words proved it. 'You promised me a tour of the land,' she reminded him, giving the impression that the wealth of feeling pent-up inside her needed a far bigger space if it was ever to run free. 'Do you think we could talk as we tour?'

'The Jeep?'

She frowned. 'Horseback?'

'You ride?'

'Tom taught me,' Sienna explained with a wistful smile as she thought back.

He could have kicked himself. Of course, Tom had taught her to ride. 'Your brother was an excellent rider. He often used to sub for our polo team. Why don't we go to the stable, and I'll match you with a suitable mount?'

'High-spirited and temperamental?' Sienna suggested deadpan.

It was the smallest spark of humour, but he'd take it. 'I'll find you something gentle and biddable.'

'You wish,' Sienna replied.

CHAPTER ELEVEN

SIENNA WAS AN accomplished rider, and formed an immediate bond with the pony he'd chosen. 'But you should slow down,' he objected when they eventually reined in at a spectacular viewing point that could never have been reached by Jeep.

'Do you mean because of the baby? Relax. I'm pregnant, not sick,' she said, dismounting. 'What a view! What a place. No wonder you and Tom loved the island so much. My brother was always a romantic, but I can't think of anyone who'd remain unmoved by this. Oh, wait,' she said with a teasing glance at him.

'Okay. You got me,' he said as he sprang down to join her. 'I love this island.'

'You can't hide it,' she said.

'I don't want to hide it,' he admitted to his own surprise. If Sienna stayed on the island, he hoped she'd come to love it as much as he did.

'Do you know what I'd like to hear about?' he said as he leaned back against a tree.

'Is this a guessing game?'

Responding to her sideways smile, he said, 'No. I'd like you to tell me more about the Tom I didn't know—your big brother.'

'He was the best—the most fun, the most caring, the most adorable, loving big brother anyone could have. Tom always threw the best parties too. I guess he was trying to make up for the fact that our parents weren't there to do things like that for either of us. He did get a little wild at times,' she remembered with a frown. 'One time Tom hired circus performers and insisted on going up on the trapeze with them. He used to terrify me with some of his stunts, but, being Tom, he somehow got away with it.'

Not that last time, he thought.

'And you?' she pressed, turning to stare at him. 'What about you, Alejandro? You used to come here with your family before...' Her voice tailed away as she stopped short of reminding him that everything had changed when his parents were killed.

'We used to have great times here,' he admitted. 'We stayed in a simple ranch house—the same one Tom left you. Boys slept in the attic, while Sofia, often as not, slept in the stable with the kittens. We'd ride bareback for hours, and tumble off exhausted at the end of the day. As the oldest I had to keep everyone in check, and that was no easy task, I can tell you, but somehow we managed to survive: riding, swimming and skiing until we dropped, in between picnicking, thanks to Maria, to our hearts' content.'

'You make it sound like paradise.'

'It was.' But now it was time to return to practicalities. Exposing his innermost feelings like this was new to him and took some getting used to. 'The river divides our land,' he explained. 'Your land is on the left, as we look at the river, with mine on the right.'

'With nary a bridge in between?' Sienna suggested, raising a brow as she looked at him.

He refused to be drawn, and, remounting his horse, he informed her that they would be riding home at a sedate pace.

'If you need a gentle ride,' she said as she mounted her pony, 'I'm fine with that.'

Ignoring her light, mocking tone, he urged his horse into a steady canter. Sienna rode up alongside. 'Don't worry,' she reassured him. 'Tom taught me to always ride within my capability.'

'Did Tom also mention that horses are unpredictable?'

'Anyone would think you were concerned about me,' she remarked with an amused grin.

'Of course, I'm concerned about you,' he said with a frown. 'If you think for one moment I take responsibility lightly, you really don't know me at all.'

'That's just it, isn't it?' Sienna replied. 'We don't know each other, and we should have discussed our plans for the future long before this. But—if I'm allowed to make an observation— I'd say things are improving, and we're both opening up.'

'One step at a time?' he suggested.

'Something like that,' she agreed, turning her face to the sun. Opening her eyes again, she stared him square in the face. 'Whether you accept what I'm going to say next, or not, you have shown concern for me. You chose a very kind pony, and you're in danger of relaxing. You just don't like anyone to imagine you've got a heart.'

'Concentrate on riding,' he advised. Just in time, as it turned out.

A snake hissed and Sienna's pony shied.

Reacting on instinct, he whipped her out of the saddle and seated her in front of him before she had chance to protest.

'There—that proves I'm right,' she insisted as he snapped a lead rein on her pony. 'Caring is second nature to you, so, however harsh you try to appear, you can never quite bring it off.'

'With a baby to think about, of course I care.'

'Our baby will always come first,' she agreed.
'It will,' he confirmed, riding on.

Had she made a breakthrough? Sienna wondered as they rode on. Whatever had happened,
or not happened, between them since they'd first
met, Alejandro made her feel safe. Sex alone
would never be enough for her. For Sienna, the
intimacy of closeness meant everything. It was
like a tiny green shoot she had to nurture and
see grow. Both she and Alejandro were stubborn, and they had been unyielding, but maybe
in time that could change. The challenge that
was Alejandro was what she found so attractive
about him, but if only he could extend the care
he showed others to himself.

He reined in beside the river that divided their
land. Could anything bridge that span? she wondered as she stared at the rushing water. Alejandro and Tom had been happy to share the island,
so why couldn't she? 'Is that Tom's farmhouse?'
she asked with interest.

'It was going to be,' Alejandro confirmed as
they surveyed the caved-in roof and broken-
down walls. Dismounting, he held out his arms
to help her down. 'We had intended to rebuild
it together.'

'Together?' she said, staring up as he lifted
her down. 'Don't you mean that you would do

the grunt work, while Tom lay on the grass dreaming, when he wasn't issuing the occasional order?'

'Is that any way to speak about your brother?' Alejandro asked in a disturbing, teasing murmur as he held her a hair's breadth away from his mouth.

'I speak the truth,' she whispered back. 'You know I do.'

He'd paused in the act of lifting her down, which resulted in a slow slide down the length of his hard body. By the time she was steady on her feet again, she was lost to reason, but Alejandro stepped back. 'I promised to help Tom with all the repairs, and as far as I'm concerned nothing has changed. I'll do the same for you.'

They were both sad that Tom hadn't lived to see his dream come to fruition, but they still had time to make things right. She said so.

'I hope you're right,' Alejandro admitted. 'One thing's certain,' he added as they each mounted their own horse. 'I'm glad about the baby. You need to hear that.'

'Yes, I do.'

One step at a time, Sienna thought as she settled back into the saddle. 'This has been a lot for both of us—Tom's death, me inheriting his land, and now we're having a baby. I just want you to know, I won't hold you to anything—'

'Stop,' Alejandro advised. 'Good news has the power to heal grief, and we have great news. Give that chance to sink in.'

'Chance to heal?' she suggested with both longing and hope.

Alejandro's long stare confirmed her belief that they'd grown closer during the ride. One step at a time, indeed, she thought, smiling back.

When they had dismounted in the yard, Alejandro explained that there was a new horse he wanted to trial. 'Leaving you free to do as you like for the rest of the evening.'

With a smile, she left him. Walking into the kitchen to see Maria's cheerful face turned her growing optimism into certainty. How could anything go wrong with Maria around? They chatted for a while, and then Sienna excused herself to go upstairs to her bedroom. Her room overlooked what Maria described as the home paddock, explaining this was where Alejandro trained his horses.

A quick shower later, Sienna was standing by the window, on the pretext of drying her hair with a towel, when actually she was staring at Alejandro. Could there be a better sight than this man in snug-fitting breeches? Calf-length, close-fitting riding boots teamed with a form-fitting black top completed the picture of male perfection. A red bandana held his wild black hair out of his eyes, and the stubble on his cheeks had grown so thick, he looked more like a marauding barbarian than a smooth tech billionaire. A glint of gold in his ear made her smile. If Alejandro had needed anything more to convince her that he was exactly the type of man any sensible woman should avoid, that earring said it all. He was unconventional. And exciting.

Now she realised something else. When it came to dealing with animals, Alejandro appeared to be transformed. He was patient and measured, endlessly gentle and kind. It was hard to believe that this was the same man she'd first met in London. Soothing his horse with long sweeping strokes down the length of its neck resulted in the half-wild stallion resting its head on his shoulder. It was at this point he looked up. Had he sensed her watching him? She shouldn't forget that working with animals tuned people's senses to an acute degree.

None of that would have mattered if she hadn't been wearing sexy silk pyjamas. Who could resist plundering that new supply of clothes? She'd ended up selecting something totally inappropriate to wear for a long, solo night on a rural ranch, but they felt so amazing next to her skin.

Turning away from the window, she stared at her reflection in the mirror. It was like staring at a stranger. The sensual slither of silk against her shower-warm skin reminded her of Alejandro's feathering touches. Turning her head, she looked at him again, only to find him looking back at her. She held his gaze boldly with a question in her eyes. Was this the sort of bedroom attire he was accustomed to women wearing? Was that why his PA had chosen such provocative nightwear?

Resisting the temptation to shred the glorious garments at the thought of other women flaunting themselves in front of Alejandro, she accepted the harsh truth: she wanted him to see her like this. She wanted him to find her irresistible. Playing with fire was dangerous, but it was also dangerously appealing.

The sight of Sienna in upmarket lingerie took him completely by surprise. Framed in an upstairs window, she looked like a goddess with her glorious auburn hair cascading in gleaming waves to her waist. The colour of the silk against her skin looked amazing. The soft cream and gold enhanced her luminous beauty, making it dangerously easy to imagine the flimsy fabric brushing intimately against every part of her.

Aroused? He was in agony.

Sheer effort of will allowed him to return his attention to the horse. Control was everything, but training would soon be over, and then it would be time to set the horse free. There was always a balance to be struck between managing and spoiling the spirit of a beautiful animal. Respect on both sides was vital. Trust equally so. Would it ever be possible to achieve that same fine balance with Sienna? Could he commit to a relationship without losing control of his heart?

'Hey,' he murmured to the horse as he removed its head collar. 'It's time for you to run free.'

She rang down to let Maria know that she wouldn't be joining Alejandro for dinner.

'Relax,' Maria insisted. 'If you're changed and ready for bed, snuggle up and let your cares float away.'

If only it were that easy, Sienna thought ruefully as images of Alejandro in the saddle, where he belonged, made her mouth dry and her body yearn. 'It's been so long since I rode a horse, my muscles are screaming,' she explained. 'I'm not sure I could even make it down the stairs.'

'Well, you don't have to try.'

There was something in Maria's voice that said she didn't believe a word of Sienna's excuse, but, with her usual diplomacy, she let it pass.

Missing dinner led to brooding on her own. Switching off the light allowed moonlight to flood the room. The setting was painfully romantic, but without a romantic hero it was a waste. As her mood took a downturn, it wasn't long before the plans she'd made in London, to build a treatment facility on the island, seemed over-ambitious, even reckless. What made her think she could take half an island, build on it, live on it, run a business *and* bring up a child, and do all of that successfully? What was her track record in the commercial world? Tom had paid for her singing lessons, and Jason had been at her side during every professional gig.

Why don't you give up right now? Sienna's inner critic suggested.

The only sure path to failure was giving up. She had to reason things out. Her biggest hurdle was Alejandro and the way he made her feel. Did he still want her? Was he only keeping her here because of their child? Business challenges turned out to be the least of her worries.

So, what are you going to do about it?

'Me?' She actually spoke the word out loud.

I don't see anyone else sitting on the bed, feeling sorry for themself.

It was a relief to hear a tap on the door as Maria arrived with a tray of food. 'I can't let you go hungry,' the housekeeper insisted, adding a stern instruction for Sienna to eat.

What was she hiding away from? What did she hope to achieve? She picked at her food. It was delicious, of course, but she had no appetite. Pushing the tray to one side, she climbed into bed. The irony of wearing silk pyjamas wasn't lost on her. They might feel amazing, but who would see them, touch them, peel them off?

Thoughts continued to whirl in her head, expanding like ripples on a pond. Being pregnant with Alejandro's baby was the most wonderful gift, and he'd been right to say that the island was the perfect place to raise a child. Maria's smiling face came into her mind. There'd be so much support here…

Inhaling deeply on the scent of freshly picked flowers, she felt their soothing presence on the dressing table like a warm hug, and, with the first sigh of contentment she'd uttered in a very long time, she snuggled down beneath the covers, and quickly fell asleep.

She dreamed about Tom. Her brother was

talking to her, and encouraging her to give the island a chance, and stay. He didn't seem at all alarmed she'd arrived by such unconventional means. Quite the opposite, in fact; he seemed thrilled and happy that she was pregnant with Alejandro's child.

Did you plan this? Is that why I'm here?

But the dream was already fading, and, as hard as she tried to hold onto it, Tom vanished. For the first time since the officers had brought her the terrible news, she woke up and cried for her brother. It was a long time before she fell silent again, but when she did it was with the certainty that Tom would always be safe in her memory, while Alejandro was safe in her heart.

He heard Sienna crying as he passed her room on his way to bed. He wouldn't intrude on private grief, though her sadness moved something deep inside him. The loss of a friend like Tom would stay with him for ever. He knew there were strategies to help deal with loss, but had chosen to distance himself from all relief. He was too busy—there were too many calls on his time for him to sit around grieving. But Sienna's tears could not be ignored. He found it impossible to distance himself from that.

Alone in bed, he turned out the light, but he couldn't sleep, and he couldn't relax. It was back to the old dilemma. Could he give Sienna everything she needed? The thought of anyone else trying to made him more restless still. What did she want out of life? They'd already established that she didn't want his money, his power, or any of the more obvious things.

She needs love.

Was he the man to give her the love she craved, or would he back away when things got heavy, as he always had before? Remaining remote had allowed him to skirt around meaningful involvement, but Sienna was different, she was unique, but that didn't make the problem go away, it only made it worse. Staring at the ceiling, he eventually fell into a restless, troubled sleep.

They sat in silence over breakfast the next day. The chat she'd planned didn't happen. It was impossible to start a conversation with Alejandro in this mood. Closed off didn't even begin to describe how he was this morning. He barely acknowledged her presence at the table, and ate with studied concentration, as if breakfast was a chore to get through before the real business of the day could begin.

'Ready?' he demanded, startling her into full attention.

'For…?'

'Settling our affairs, of course. The land?' he prompted.

She didn't move as he left the table. 'As far as I'm concerned, the land is a secondary consideration.'

'For you, perhaps.' He stood, waiting by the door. 'We can talk on the way,' he insisted.

'On the way to where?'

'To show you your boundaries, of course.'

Someone had got out of bed the wrong side. 'The land can wait,' she said calmly. 'It isn't going anywhere, while our child—'

'What about our child?' he said, coming back to plant his fists on the table. 'I don't see there's anything to discuss where the baby's concerned. You'll live here. Maria will help you. What more could you ask? When the child's older, Maria's daughter runs an excellent play scheme, and there are several excellent schools on the island—'

'Do you intend to live here too?'

'Well, I—'

'Exactly,' she said, standing to confront him. 'You haven't decided. You'll do as you please, as always, I imagine. And, as for education, don't you think it's a little soon to be discussing our child's schooling?'

'Never,' Alejandro countered with passion.

'Education is the most important element in a child's life.'

'So is love, care, support, and happiness,' Sienna argued fiercely.

'I don't understand your problem,' Alejandro admitted as they fired angry looks at each other.

'I'll tell you what my problem is. I feel as if you've made a decree, and I have to fall into line. I thought we were getting somewhere yesterday. I thought we were close. But that's just it, isn't it, Alejandro? You can't bear to get too close to anyone, so you've stepped away before that can happen. You're allowed to talk and express opinions, but you expect me to listen without comment. I'm not allowed to interfere, because you've taken over something we should be planning together. Control is great sometimes, but you can't control me, or use control as an excuse to ignore your emotions.'

'That has never been my intention,' he said stiffly.

'Then, bend a little,' she begged. 'Look to the future, as I do, to when we have a new life to consider.'

'I have many businesses to run, and endless calls on my time—'

'So, you'll be too busy to take an interest in your child?'

Alejandro made a sound of exasperation as he raked his hair.

'Sit, talk, discuss the future with me. Give some of your time, Alejandro. Our baby deserves that much, at least. Think of the benefits if we work together. Two people at war can't hope to achieve anything. I'm not saying we have to live together, but we must raise our child together.'

'Continents apart?'

'Even then,' she said steadily.

Several long, tense moments passed as they stared at each other unblinking, until finally Sienna broke the silence. It wasn't the conversation she's planned, but at least seeing the island would be better than this tension. 'When you're ready, I actually would like to take another look at the land. We've both got a lot to think about, and I don't want to rush into an uninformed decision.'

'Are you planning to leave the island?'

There was real concern in his voice.

'I don't know yet,' she said honestly.

Whatever the outcome between them, she would go it alone, if she had to. She'd raise her child with love and live happily, while somehow finding a way to bring Tom's dream to fruition.

CHAPTER TWELVE

THEY HAD ACHIEVED a truce of sorts, and that had to be enough for now. At least they could talk without trying to score points or remain stubbornly standing on their dignity. They were as bad as one another, Sienna mused as she accompanied Alejandro outside again. Butting heads was putting it mildly. 'The solicitor gave me a map,' she reminded him as they crossed the stable yard. 'I've marked a few places in red—places I'm particularly interested in...'

He paused mid-stride.

'Before you take me to see them, please accept that this isn't about money for me. It's more about building a life.'

'Everything's about money,' he said with a frown.

'If you believe that, I feel sorry for you,' she called after him. 'You can't just make the rules and expect everyone else to live by them.

I might be in your world right now, but I insist on having a say.'

'You insist?' he called over his shoulder.

'Yes, I do. Did your father put money before love?' she demanded, catching him up. 'You told me about your wonderful childhood with loving parents, who always wanted the best for their children. Has something changed since then? Are you concerned that you will never be able to live up to your parents' example?'

'My child will lack for nothing,' he barked, increasing his stride and the distance between them. 'I promise you that.'

'If you give your children everything,' she said, jogging alongside, 'what will they have to strive for?'

'Children? Do you intend to have more?'

His gaze was harsh, but she held it steadily. 'Who knows what the future holds?'

'You apparently know more than me. Well?' he queried in the same harsh tone. 'Do you want to see this land, or not?'

'I do,' she confirmed.

'We'll take the Jeep to save time.'

She didn't argue, having sensed that Alejandro's mood was already easing. He wasn't a bad man, he was a man coming face to face with an argumentative nemesis, and for that she could only feel glad. Alejandro had always taken charge of everything, but now he had a helpmate in the mother of his child.

'Would you be interested to hear about my plans?'

'Very much so.'

Her spirits lifted at Alejandro's suggestion. This wasn't a small step. It was a giant leap in the right direction. *'Vamos!'* she said, smiling as he leaned in front of her to open the passenger door of the Jeep.

'One proviso…'

'Which is?' she asked, turning to face him.

'We can't be late for Tom's party.'

Her heart beat a furious tattoo at Alejandro's use of the word *we*. She didn't want to read too much into it, but it felt good. 'Maria's gone to a lot of trouble,' she agreed. 'We won't be late. I'm sure you'll see to that.'

Before they left Maria caught sight of them, and as always his housekeeper was fully prepared. 'Here's some food for your picnic,' she said, racing up to the Jeep.

'That's very kind of you,' Sienna said, leaning across him, delivering warmth and scent and womanliness to his starving senses. 'We won't be late back,' she promised with a smile.

He parked up on the riverbank, where they had a good view of both parcels of land.

'This is perfect,' Sienna said when they'd laid out the picnic.

'It's the exact spot where I used to come with my family,' he revealed. 'My parents used to set out a picnic beneath this very tree. If you look over there,' he said, pointing to where building work had already started, 'you can see where I'm building Tom's retreat for veterans.'

'You're building Tom's retreat,' Sienna echoed thoughtfully.

'It's been a long time in the planning. It will overlook the river on one side and the mountains on the other.'

'Which sounds perfect,' she agreed.

He could see her thinking, how could one small island house two similar facilities? The answer was, it couldn't, but, being Sienna, she put her own hopes and dreams to one side and thought only of the benefits for others.

'It's going to be wonderful,' she said, smiling with sincerity into his eyes.

Her hair was loose and blowing free, and her cheeks were already pinking up in the sun. Understated appeal had truthfully never interested him before, but that was before he met Sienna.

'I wonder,' she said as she brought a cup of juice to her lips.

'You wonder what?' he pressed.

'Could we work together? It makes sense,

doesn't it? You're building a retreat, and I want to build a music therapy centre. Why can't we combine the two? I'd have to renovate Tom's house first, of course,' she said, frowning as she developed her plan, 'but once that was habitable and I moved in, we could allocate some of the rooms in your facility for music therapy. Couldn't we?' she added hopefully.

He wondered if she knew how appealing she was, but had she really considered everything in detail as he had? 'Do you intend to keep on working when you have the baby?'

'Of course. Why not?'

'Because I imagine you'll be fully occupied bringing up our child.'

'I won't stop being me when our baby's born,' she protested. 'I'm a qualified music therapist. I can help people. I won't allow my studies to go to waste.'

Alejandro was frowning but she could tell he was listening. 'Tom taught me the importance of independence when our parents were killed, and that's a lesson I've never forgotten.'

But it was more than that, Sienna realised. She had to work. She would always work, because love could be ripped away, while music was something that no one could take away from her. Her insecurities were showing, she accepted, but Tom had sacrificed so much to pay for Sienna to advance her studies. She couldn't imagine he'd be pleased if she gave up both her career and her self-determination the moment Alejandro came into her life.

She continued, 'Didn't you admit that playing the piano offered you a form of escape? Music heals, Alejandro. We both know that. Why shouldn't our child grow up knowing that too? I plan for our baby to accompany me. The first thing I'm going to do is create a crèche within the facility, so that mothers can be close to their children.'

Alejandro's hum suggested he liked the idea, but he was still frowning. 'As the child's father, I can promise you that you'll never have to work another day in your life.'

'Is that supposed to make me happy?' she asked with a sad smile. 'I'm sure it would sound attractive to some, but I want to work. I don't want to be treated like one of your brood mares, pampered and cared for until the day our baby is born, at which point, according to your reasoning, I'll be superfluous to requirements, and likely dismissed.'

'Your reasoning is wrong.'

'A woman defending her child is wrong? Why can't we both work, and still give our child all the love in the world? Alejandro?' she pressed. 'What's really behind your concern? Are you afraid you'll never be able to replicate your own happy childhood? Honestly, I sometimes think I have more faith in you than you have in yourself.'

'Replicating my childhood is a big ask.'

'Mine too, but I'm determined to do it. Will you join me?'

He said nothing for a long while, and then admitted, 'If you met my sister and brothers, you might realise that the great wealth you fear so much isn't necessarily a burden, but an opportunity to do good.'

'I'd really like that, and I hope I get the chance. I only have to see your face light up when you talk about your family to know you must have deep feelings locked away somewhere. You have to set those feelings free. I'm the first to admit that isn't easy, but it's possible, and the next step is to learn to care about yourself.'

Alejandro Acosta, forced to climb down by an outstanding woman? Guilty as charged. If he lost her—if he lost Sienna's trust—that was the worst he could imagine.

'Let's toss ideas around,' she suggested. 'We can argue and reason, until finally you accept that—'

'You know best?' he suggested with the hint of a smile.

'Until you accept that I can be a good mother, and do other things too,' she said, smiling warmly into his eyes.

All he wanted was to be close to this woman. He wanted them to understand each other, and to trust each other, and for Sienna to realise that his wealth was no barrier to happiness. To convince her, he would first have to prove to her that the power he wielded would never be used to control her.

As if reading his mind, she smiled and touched his arm. 'I've never doubted your sense of responsibility, Alejandro. I just don't want to be crushed by it.'

Their stares locked and held in mutual understanding. They'd got a lot off their chests, opening the door to more discussion. By the time they swapped conversation for food, great strides had been made. 'After you,' he insisted.

'Oh, no, after you,' Sienna countered with a grin. 'I can wait.'

To hell with that!

'I can't,' he said, dragging her close.

It was like a first kiss, intense, searching, and beautiful. When they eventually parted, it was as if they couldn't bear to move more than a breath away. Alejandro's fierce gaze warm and reassuring. Was she still hoping for too much?

Kissing her again, he made it easy to stay in his arms. Maybe she didn't pull back as soon as she should, but there was still a moment, even at the point of no return, when questions forced their way into her mind. 'You want to ask me about Tom,' Alejandro guessed, when she failed to put her thoughts into words.

'Only because I can sense when you're holding back,' she said. 'I know you want to protect me, but I'm stronger than you know, and I'm asking you not to. I want to see Tom as you knew him.'

Alejandro paused, and countless expressions flashed behind his eyes, as if he was battling his own demons. 'We were similar in some ways,' he said at last. 'Neither of us could forgive ourselves for our parents' deaths. The fact that Tom, like me, had nothing to do with it has never counted, because guilt is a strange animal. It can drive you to believe that you could have done something, or that you *should* have done something, and that if you had, you might have saved them. Tom once told me that the only reason he carried on living was to protect you.'

'I wish Tom had tried harder to stay alive.'

'So do I.'

As Alejandro fell silent she felt guilty for pressing him.

'Thinking back isn't easy,' he said at last.

'I'm sure not,' she agreed softly. 'I'm guessing you won't give me the detail, but I can still work it out. Tom tempted fate once too often. He liked to taunt fate.'

'Because Tom saw fate as being unfair to him,' Alejandro said, quick to excuse his friend. 'You're right, he took a risk that night that cost him his life. As for telling you more? I don't see there's anything to be gained by that. I'm not even sure there is more—at least, nothing that would help you.'

'You don't like to lie, and you don't like to pile on the pain,' she observed with a wry twist of her mouth.

'Why would I do either of those things?'

Leave it. They'd both suffered the most terrible grief. Who would want to revisit that? She started to clear up their picnic as a cover for threatening tears. 'I don't want to upset you. I'll just say that, whenever you remember something you can tell me about Tom—happy times, playing polo, maybe—you tell me more about the Tom I didn't know.'

'Tom was brave—the bravest man in the regiment.'

After his reticence on the subject of Tom, Alejandro's words shocked her. 'Brave, or foolhardy?'

He turned his head away briefly, as if to acknowledge the distinction, then turned back to her, to state firmly, 'Tom was brave in so many ways.'

That told Sienna more about her brother than a thousand words. Tom's impulsive phases, back when they were living together, his countless reckless actions. It had all been there under her nose, but she hadn't seen it—

'Don't feel guilty, Sienna. I can read you. You've seen what guilt does. It's corrosive. Fight it off. Move on. Move forward. You know that's what Tom would want.'

'You're right,' she conceded, firming her jaw. 'I guess this is why Tom talked about you all the time. He relied on your judgement.'

A faint sad smile touched Alejandro's mouth. 'Your brother talked about you all the time. He was so proud of you and your beautiful voice.'

'Yet now, I wonder if I even knew him.'

Alejandro shrugged. 'Did anyone know Tom? Like the rest of us, your brother was a complex character.'

'Which is why you tiptoe around the truth.'

She was right. No one had truly known Tom; not the psychiatrist who treated him, his sister, Sienna, not even Alejandro. The light-hearted man Sienna described was a front Tom adopted when it suited him. Guilt had ruled Tom to the point where he took far too many risks, as if inviting fate to notice *him*. 'If you're asking me, did your brother have mental health issues? Yes, he did.'

'And you covered for him,' she suggested.

They had all covered for Tom. Believing him when he said he was getting better. Not realising how ill he was until it was far too late. It was something Alejandro would never forgive himself for. When breakdowns happened in the heat of battle, there were no convenient committees to decide if someone needed to be medevacced out.

Seeing the pain in her eyes, he couldn't tell Sienna that. She'd lost a brother, which was bad enough, and was pregnant, which was another life-changing event. The last thing he wanted was to add to her pain. 'Tom meant a lot to me. We were as close as brothers. I'd have done anything for him, which is why I know Tom would want you to enjoy this pregnancy, and not feel guilty for being happy.'

'He would have been a fun uncle, don't you think?'

'Yes, I do,' he agreed. It might even have been the saving of him. They'd never know. 'The best way to honour Tom's memory is to embrace every moment, as he would, with optimism and energy.'

'That's such a lovely thing to say.'

Drawing her into his arms, he kissed her brow. 'Tom's probably looking down right now, and agreeing with me that you will be a great mother.'

'He was certainly a great brother. He never missed a parents' evening, and somehow found time to teach to me to ride, to drive, and so many other things.' Lifting her head, she searched his eyes with distress. 'And all that, while he was sick. I wish he'd been more open. I'd have found help. There are so many people waiting to offer support.'

'You, for instance.'

'Me?'

'Now you're a fully trained music therapist,' Alejandro reminded her.

She had to turn away. The irony of her vocation had never struck Sienna before, but now it did, and forcefully. 'I could have helped Tom.'

'You did help Tom,' Alejandro insisted. 'You gave him unconditional love, and now Tom's legacy will live on through you. No one should feel alone, and we can all play a small part in letting people know that support is available.'

'You're so wise,' she said quietly, then, turning to him, she added, 'Do you think Tom planned this all along?'

'Planned what? Throwing us together?' Alejandro smiled as he shrugged. 'Maybe he threw the dice, but he couldn't know where it would land.'

That made three of them, Sienna guessed as Alejandro picked up the picnic basket and they headed back to the car.

CHAPTER THIRTEEN

ALEJANDRO HAD MADE a lot of things clearer, Sienna reflected as they drove back to the ranch, but one thing still troubled her. If Alejandro had known Tom was sick, had he allowed Tom to go forward into danger? Was Alejandro responsible for Tom's death?

If she could be reasonable for ten seconds together, she might accept that this was an overreaction, produced by raging pregnancy hormones, all mixed up with her old friend doubt.

She needed to be alone to think things through, and the moment they reached the ranch house, she leapt out of the vehicle before Alejandro had chance to help her down. The sight of Maria arranging trestle tables for the party brought her up short in the yard. How could she take herself off when Maria was working so hard to make Tom's party a success?

Holding out her arms to Sienna, Maria welcomed her back. 'I hope you had a good picnic?'

'Wonderful, thanks to you.' The food had been great, the company too, it was just those unanswered questions plaguing her. All the more so because Alejandro was still close by.

But not for long.

'You'll excuse me,' he said.

'Of course,' Sienna chorused with Maria.

'I've saved the vital final touches for you—' Maria broke off, to take a closer look at Sienna. 'Is something wrong?'

Maria could never be fooled. 'Nothing,' Sienna insisted with an unconvincing laugh.

'Go back to the house,' Maria instructed gently. 'You've had a long, hot morning, and should take a shower and have a rest.'

'And your morning has been cool and easy?' Sienna said.

'This is what I do,' Maria exclaimed with a happy gesture that encompassed the entire yard. 'Go,' she encouraged warmly.

The cool of the house was a relief. Sienna's thoughts were in such a muddle that a shower seemed like the best idea. A quick change of clothes later, and she hurried back to the vast cobbled yard to join Maria. If there was anyone who could tell her more about Tom, Alejandro's warm-hearted housekeeper was that person.

Maria's face softened the moment Sienna mentioned Tom's name. 'He was such a lovely young man,' she reminisced with a wistful look on her face. 'Always helpful, always smiling—' She paused there, to look at Sienna with concern. 'I was surprised when Alejandro explained that he had brought Tom to the island, to help him...recover.'

'Recover?' Sienna pressed carefully.

Maria gave a heavy sigh. 'There were two sides to your brother: the charming, happy man who couldn't do enough for you, and the tormented soul who troubled us all. Seeing those contrasts in action gave me some insight into how badly Tom had been damaged in battle.'

'You're not talking about physical injuries, are you?'

'No,' Maria confirmed. Compassion filled her eyes. 'I'm sorry, Sienna, didn't you know about this?'

'Alejandro has told me a few things, but he always draws back. I think he's frightened of upsetting me.'

'Of course, he is, and he doesn't want to add to the needless guilt you're suffering. Alejandro knows how you feel, because he suffers in exactly the same way. You have to stop punishing yourself, Sienna, just as he does. Survivor's guilt is normal. Once you've accepted that, you're halfway to learning strategies that will allow you to move on.'

There was a long pause, and then Sienna asked the question pressing on her mind. 'Can you tell me anything more about Tom?'

Maria paused in putting a tray down on the table. Turning to face Sienna, she admitted, 'He was very good at hiding his illness. Some scars are invisible, some are not, but Alejandro sees everything. I believe that's why he gave your brother half this island—'

'Alejandro *gave* Tom half the island?' Shock ripped through Sienna. 'Do you mean, there was no payment involved?'

'None at all.' Maria's dark eyes searched Sienna's face. 'I don't suppose Alejandro told you that?'

'He certainly didn't,' Sienna confirmed. 'My understanding was that they bought the island together.' She frowned. 'Or that maybe Alejandro bought it, and then agreed to sell half the land to Tom.'

'I can understand how you might think that,' Maria admitted. 'Who else on earth has Alejandro's level of wealth? I realise it's hard to imagine. It's hard for me, and I live in the same house as him. *Buying* an island. *Giving* half an island away. These are regular kindnesses for Alejandro. But I think it was more than that, because Alejandro was always convinced this land possessed healing properties, and if your brother spent enough time here, it would heal him. I do know he begged Tom to find help. He thought he was getting better.'

Alejandro had tried to protect her brother, as he was now offering his protection to Sienna.

Seeing the turmoil in her eyes, Maria advised, 'You must try to remember the good times with your brother, because that's what Tom would want you to do.'

'I wish I could, but I've had terrible thoughts about Alejandro—'

'Haven't we all?' Maria interrupted with a rueful laugh. 'But know this,' she said. 'Alejandro has never backed down from a challenge. He's the best and most loyal of men, which is why he is everyone's hero, and why he's so loved on this island. Tonight's celebration of Tom will mean a great deal to Alejandro, as it does to all of us who knew your brother, and I know it means everything to you.'

'More than you know,' Sienna agreed.

'And the best way to honour Tom is to laugh and sing and dance,' Maria said, giving Sienna a hug. 'Live your life to the full,' she instructed, pulling back. 'Celebrate the brother you remember, as we all will.'

'Tom did love a good party,' Sienna admitted.

'Well, then…' Maria jerked her chin in the

direction of the house. 'We're finished here. Go and get ready for the party.'

'I'll be back as soon as I can.'

'No hurry. Everything's under control,' Maria assured her. 'Why don't you go for a relaxing swim? Give your emotions chance to settle down. I promise to leave the finishing touches to you.'

In a very different mood, Sienna turned to go, and missed the shrewd expression sparking in Maria's eyes.

Space from Sienna had allowed him to sort out his thoughts. Seeing her eyes so full of concern had proved that, in trying to avoid hurting her, by editing the truth about Tom, he'd only succeeded in hurting her more. What good would it do to add to her pain by telling her that by disobeying his order to remain in camp until further instruction Tom had risked, not only his own life on that dreadful night, but the lives of all his comrades too?

By the time he reached the gym he was wound up tight. Binding his fists, he took out his frustration on the heavy bag. The only thought that saved him was that Sienna was pregnant with his child. A few weeks ago, he would have thought it impossible for that to take precedence over everything else. He'd come a long way since Sienna had kick-started his emotions. One thing was very clear in his mind, as he slammed his fist into the bag: the role of part-time parent would never be enough for him.

And Sienna?

She was the first person ever to interfere with his plans and scheduling. Unleashing a fresh flurry of blows, he hammered the bag until it almost swung off the hook. Finishing with a couple of punishing roundhouse kicks, he stood back panting, fists clenched, brow lowered. And still the fire inside him refused to go out.

Stripping off his wrist bands and clothes in the changing room, he took a cold shower. No water was cold enough to refresh both body and mind when he was in this mindset. Towelling down roughly, he dragged on a pair of swimming shorts before bulldozing his way through the doors to the pool. He stopped dead. Sienna was there before him.

'I hope you don't mind,' she called out as she pulled herself onto the side.

'Not at all,' he snapped, turning to go.

Too late. She somehow waylaid him, and now she stood, looking like an improvement on Botticelli's Venus. How was it possible for Sienna to be even more beautiful each time he saw her?

She launched straight in. 'Maria told me

about the island—about the arrangement you made with Tom. Seems I owe you an apology.'

'Oh?'

'Maria explained that you hoped your gift would heal my brother, which makes me guilty of misunderstanding you, and I'm sorry for that. Turns out there's a lot I don't know about Tom.'

'Save the guilt. There's been too much of that. Any questions you have, I'll try to answer.'

'I'm guessing you won't try too hard.'

'You might be right,' he said bluntly.

What was Maria up to? She'd known where he'd be. Best guess? His wily housekeeper had sent Sienna on ahead. But why? To soothe him? To put things straight? Or was this straightforward matchmaking, by a lovely, if rather misguided woman?

That thought was enough to force him to turn his back on the sight of Señorita Slater, half naked in a provocative swimming costume, no doubt chosen by his PA. 'You don't have to leave just because I'm going,' he said.

'But I do,' Sienna protested. 'I promised Maria I'd help her with the final touches.'

Reasonably content that his body was back under control, he swung around in time to see Sienna styling her hair into a messy up-do. The action pressed her breasts together. There was only so much torture he could take in one day.

Taking evasive action, he plunged into the pool with relief.

To be continued, he reflected as he powered through the water. They weren't anywhere near done. He wanted Sienna, in every way there was. He'd even marry her, if that was what it took to keep both Sienna and their child close.

Would that be such a bad thing?

What to wear for the party, when all she could think about was the touch of Alejandro's lips on her mouth—and, of course, would he ever kiss her again?

Come on, hurry up! Maria's waiting.

Choosing a simple, knee-length fit and flare, in a vivid shade of fuchsia pink, she left her hair to flow wild and free around her shoulders.

Was wild and free the look she should be aiming for?

Why not? Mother-to-be, soon-to-be business-woman, musician, and Tom's very proud sister would definitely choose provocative pink. Slipping her feet into flat, strappy sandals, she added a touch of lip gloss and a spritz of scent before hurrying out of the room.

She worked well with Maria, and they'd soon finished the final decoration of the tables, adding white flowers and a sprinkle of silver glitter to each centrepiece. 'I think we can call that a success,' Sienna declared, standing back with her friend to admire their handiwork.

'I couldn't agree more.'

Sienna's body tingled at the sound of Alejandro's voice. He was standing right behind her. All the tiny hairs on the back of her neck lifted, and, as if by magic, Maria took the hint, and left them to it.

'You okay?' Alejandro probed, when she remained with her back turned.

Apart from a bad case of Alejandro fever, yes, she was fine. 'Yes, thank you,' she said with a smile, turning to face him. This man was Tom's best friend, and Maria trusted Alejandro. Why couldn't she just come out with it, and say how she felt about him? Was she still frightened she might get hurt?

'Tables look great,' Alejandro observed. She and Maria had lit candles, and everything was sparkling.

'I'm surprised you noticed,' she said dryly, since Alejandro's gaze hadn't swerved from her face.

'Maria tells me we have to open the dancing,' he said.

'Is that okay with you?'

He smiled darkly. 'I might ask you the same question.'

'I think we should set a good example to

your guests.' Who were beginning to arrive in droves, Sienna noticed as Alejandro steered her towards the dance floor with his hand in the small of her back. If she closed her eyes, she could lose herself in this moment, and want nothing more out of life.

She shouldn't have been surprised to discover that Alejandro danced in the same way he made love, with flawless rhythm and perfect anticipation. When the band took a break, he suggested they head for the house, to continue their conversation.

He wouldn't give her any more detail about Tom, so she couldn't see they had anything more to talk about, but still she agreed to go with him into the house. There was a particular energy about Alejandro that she recognised. It aroused her, and explained exactly why they were leaving the party. Conversation was redundant by the time he led the way across the hall. Linking their fingers, he headed straight for the stairs. They didn't make it halfway up. 'The house is empty.' And his breath was warm on her mouth. He sounded calm, while she was not.

Those eyes. His eyes. She was lost.

In moments the dress she was wearing dropped to her feet. 'Why stand when you can sit?' Alejandro suggested as he settled her on the stairs.

Where was her next breath supposed to come from? she wondered as her remaining scraps of underwear joined her dress. 'What if Maria comes back?'

'I locked the door,' Alejandro explained with a wicked smile as he began to stroke and kiss, until, freeing himself, he brought her on top of him.

Memories didn't just stir, they roared into life. How could she have forgotten how much she needed this?

'Do you trust me?' he asked, positioning her. 'Yes.'

He filled her completely, but took his time. When she relaxed, he filled her to the hilt. Rotating his hips, he reminded her again how much she'd been missing.

Resting her head on his shoulder, she grabbed the occasional noisy breath as Alejandro brought her the pleasure she craved.

'You don't have to do anything, no need to force. Let everything happen naturally.'

She did. And lost control immediately. Tightening convulsively around him, she screamed with relief as Alejandro held her firmly in place. It took the longest time to recover, and while she was still attempting to catch enough breath he swung her into his arms. 'Bed,' he said. 'This requires my full concentration.'

That was enough to make her almost lose it again, but then she remembered the party.

'The party will go on all night,' Alejandro reassured her as he jogged up the stairs. 'Everyone's having such a good time, I doubt they'll even know we've gone.'

CHAPTER FOURTEEN

HE'D NEVER NEEDED Sienna like this. He'd never been so aroused. Stripping off the clothes she hadn't already ripped off, he stretched out beside her on the bed. Bringing her into his arms, he kissed her. Cupping her buttocks, he brought her beneath him. Moving firmly and rhythmically, he took her to the edge again. The clutch of her fingers on his shoulders, the cries from her throat, all aroused him, and she lost no opportunity to tell him exactly what she needed. 'Now,' he murmured, close to her ear when he judged the time was right.

He held her in place as she let go and didn't stop moving until he was sure she was spent. Only then did he think about claiming his own pleasure.

'That was amazing. You're amazing,' Sienna whispered. 'After so long, I never thought I'd be able to trust enough to be as uninhibited as I am with you.'

'I'm glad I make you feel safe,' he said, and, wrapping his arms around her, he kissed her again, until even he had to recognise that what had started out as savage passion had turned to something more. Sienna was the mother of his child, he reasoned. Hence his deeper feelings.

'We should get back,' she said, reminding him about the party.

Reluctantly, he agreed.

When they returned to the party, she felt frustrated that she hadn't taken the chance to have a meaningful talk about the future with Alejandro. There had been a moment when something in his eyes said he did want her for herself, not just for the moment, but she had to know that. She had to hear that. Doubts and guilt from the past could not be purged quickly, or all at once.

But even Alejandro didn't have sex out of a sense of responsibility, she reasoned as he drew her back onto the dance floor. Sex was an animal impulse that could be so much more. She wanted that 'so much more'.

Eventually, they had to leave the dance floor and circulate amongst the guests. Everyone was having such a good time, and it didn't take long to realise that Alejandro was the energy of the party, the hub around which the fun revolved. He was very different here, from that cold, aus-

tere man she'd first met in London, and all the
more attractive for it. Taking everything in, she
smiled. Tom would have loved this. She loved
this. She loved the island, the party, the bon-
fire roaring, Maria conducting everything like
the most polished maestro. Was this as close to
paradise as anyone could hope to get?

As Alejandro peeled away she went to help
Maria refill the platters on the table. Alejandro was so easy with everyone, and he looked
so relaxed and happy. He didn't seem to care
what job he took on. Opening champagne gave
him the chance to chat. When he passed around
canapés, it gave him yet another opportunity
to interact with his friends. No wonder he was
so popular on the island. It quite literally transformed him. She could only hope that it would
have the same effect on those who attended
Tom's healing facility.

Everyone wanted a piece of Alejandro, and no
wonder. Sienna did too, but she'd have to wait
for more interaction with a man who looked several degrees hotter than hell in his snug-fitting
jeans. An easy smile and open-hearted manner
gave him the magic that other people lacked.

Her cheeks fired up when she realised Alejandro had caught her staring at him and was
looking back. Lust flared between them in those

few seconds. Who else had noticed? Everyone?
Maybe, and what was wrong with that?

Doubt didn't take long to set in.

*Everyone noticed what? That you and Ale-
jandro are an item? That you're staying on the
island in his house?*

What should people make of that? Was it even
that unusual? And before she could commit herself fully to more than lust, she needed to hear
from Alejandro that what he felt for her was a
lot more than just a sense of responsibility, or
pure lust. He had to want her for herself.

Well, here's your chance, he's coming over...

He took her in, in a sweeping glance that
nearly knocked her off her feet. 'You look good,'
he remarked with a lift of his brow. 'Sex suits
you.'

'You too,' she replied calmly.

'I'm going to make an announcement,' he
said, 'and for that, you need to be at my side.'

'Why?'

He didn't answer and had already left her
side to mount the temporary stage. It must have
something to do with them working together
on the facility, she guessed as Alejandro beckoned her over.

She stood quietly by as he tapped the microphone, and was surprised when he reached for
her hand. 'I've got a really special announce-

ment,' he said. The crowd fell quiet. 'I know you'll all be thrilled to learn that Sienna, Tom Slater's sister, will be joining us here on the island.'

The cheers rang out, and he had to wait until they subsided. 'And that's not all,' he said.

As the crowd waited with bated breath, Alejandro's manner alarmed Sienna. It was as if he had returned briefly to being the cold, aloof man she remembered from their first meeting in London. He'd decided something, and nothing would sway him from his course.

What could it be? She wracked her brains for an answer. Nothing had been finalised for the music therapy centre, which, she hoped, would now be housed in the facility Alejandro was building. They hadn't even discussed working together on the project—

Forced to curtail her thoughts, she listened intently as he began, 'I've heard it said that lightning can strike, and change everything in an instant. I've never had reason to believe that before...' He turned a piercing look on her face, but instead of thrilling her, it chilled her as he added, 'I guess that lightning bolt was bound to find me eventually.'

She wasn't the only one wondering where this was leading, judging by the occasional awkward laugh.

'I won't keep you in suspense any longer,' Alejandro assured his audience. 'I'm going to ask this incredible woman to marry me.'

Somewhere in her peripheral vision, she saw Maria in shock, with her hand to her mouth. Maria wasn't the only one. Shock was pounding at Sienna's temples. Alejandro was proposing marriage in front of everyone at Tom's party, and without even asking her first?

'A few words, Sienna,' he prompted as he handed over the microphone.

Still reeling with disbelief and confusion, she had to think of her audience, all these lovely people, who only wished her well. She could do this. She had to do this.

'Thank you all for making me feel so welcome here. My brother loved a good party, and I know Tom would want us to remember him with a smile.' Love surged from the crowd, emboldening her to carry on. Careful not to make any mention of Alejandro's proposal, she said, 'I must thank Maria and Alejandro for making tonight possible, and I thank you, for your support.'

Removing the mic from her hand, Alejandro called out, 'Enjoy the party!' before he led her away.

The instant they were alone, she challenged

him. 'For goodness' sake, Alejandro, what on earth was that about?'

'My proposal of marriage?' he queried with a surprised look on his face. 'I'm being practical.'

Each of his words wounded her. But, *practical*? That was as bad as being his responsibility, if not worse. He made her feel as if that was the sum total of everything they'd been to each other—everything she had *believed* they'd been to each other, while they were making love, or when they were talking easily together, like people who trusted each other. He'd destroyed that in a few short words.

'It was as good an opportunity as any to state my intentions,' Alejandro explained with a shrug.

'It didn't occur to you, that I might like to be involved?'

'I was being spontaneous.'

'I see.'

'You don't believe me?' he said with a frown.

Actually, she did, though having allowed herself to believe Alejandro was a much-changed man, being proven wrong in the most hurtful way, had come as a shock. 'What century are you living in?' she said sadly, thinking his proposal more a tick in a box than a romantic offer.

Alejandro appeared affronted. 'I thought you'd be pleased. It's a question of security.

Surely you understand that, as the mother of my child, both you and the baby are at risk? Marrying me will give you unprecedented levels of security, as well as certainty for the future. Forgive me if I'm wrong, but I thought that was what every mother wanted?'

What about love? Where did love fit into Alejandro's grand scheme? Perhaps it didn't, Sienna concluded, too low to find the words to counter his undeniably logical explanation.

'If it's a question of money,' he said, making her start.

'That's the last thing on my mind,' she assured him with passion.

'I know. We've been through this before. I just don't want you to worry. Finances can be worked on—'

'Finances?' she repeated, as if the word tasted bitter on her tongue.

'Money, your money,' he patiently explained. 'You'll have funds from Tom's estate, as well as an allowance from me, to do with as you please.'

The word *allowance* grated. It suggested a degree of helplessness that Sienna hadn't experienced since the days before she found a way to make a living with her voice. Tom had been only too glad to support her financially, but that didn't mean she'd wanted him to, and as soon as she could be independent, she was.

'I find it hard to believe you're saying no,' Alejandro admitted with a shake of his head.

Why did people get married? Because they were better together than apart? Because everything came into clearer focus when you could see life through someone else's eyes? Shouldn't emotion be involved at some point? 'Just because you're a high-flying CEO with countless companies under your sway, doesn't mean everything has to be a deal, Alejandro. Until you change your approach—adapt it to difference circumstances—you're never going to be happy—'

'A deal?' he repeated, as if this was the only phrase that had registered.

'Yes,' Sienna insisted. 'You thought you were making a decent proposal, and so you went ahead, regardless of my opinion. Marriage means spending the rest of our lives together—agreeing, compromising, disagreeing, but finding a solution that suits us both. It isn't a company you can buy and sell when it suits you. If you go into marriage in that frame of mind, there's no certainty, and no secure foundation on which to build anything.'

'We'll have to agree to disagree,' he said, adding, 'I'll leave you to think my proposal over,' as if he was certain she'd see sense soon.

Deep, wounding hurt swept over Sienna in

successive waves as Alejandro walked away. How could she be so wrong about him? Had he never really changed from that autocratic man in London? Was she guilty of fantasising that he had, or that he would?

How could she stay here now? Tom's facility would still be built, just not here. Alejandro had so much power and money, he could create something far bigger and better on the island than Sienna could ever hope to achieve. If she had an ounce of decency in her, she'd stand back and leave him to it.

When it came to their child, there'd be no standing back. They had to come to an agreement. Placing a protective hand over her stomach, she felt with tender certainty that motherhood was a gift, and only had to think back to the happy years she'd spent with her own mother to know she was right.

She couldn't leave the party without speaking to Maria first. And there was something else she wanted to say to Alejandro—She jumped to find him behind her.

'There isn't a problem with the baby, is there?' he asked. 'Is that why you're so upset?'

'There's no problem at all,' she said levelly.

A wealth of feeling flashed behind Alejandro's eyes, to the point where she almost felt sorry for him, but he was quickly distant again.

Was she any better at showing her true feelings? Noticing Maria glancing over with concern, she made her excuses to Alejandro, and hurried over to reassure Maria.

CHAPTER FIFTEEN

SIENNA'S REFUSAL HAD shocked him. It was some distraction to mingle with his guests, but he did so like an automaton—cheery here, concerned there, without registering half the conversations. All he could think of was Sienna. All the time he looked for her, he knew he could have expressed himself better, but pretty speeches, however sincere, couldn't be learned in one night.

There had been more attempts to lure him into wedlock than he could count, and that didn't include his sister's machinations. Sofia longed for more women in the family, she'd told him. Up to meeting Sienna, he'd felt no inclination to please his sister by sharing his life with anyone. The fact that Sienna would never be a compliant wife had only added to her allure. He didn't want compliance. He wanted challenge, spark, and energy, and Sienna had those in plenty.

The odds on him recovering the situation were poor, he conceded. Wanting the one woman he couldn't have, because she had refused him, was a problem he had never thought to encounter. He should have been more open with Sienna from the start, but the day his parents were killed he'd seen how happiness could be snatched away in an instant, and he'd locked down. Trying to fill that emotional chasm with work had only proved that work wasn't enough. At family gatherings, he watched and yearned, hoping no one would guess that *Uncle* Alejandro ached for a kickabout that included his own children.

He hoped Sienna would survive his blunder. Was marriage so terrible, or just marriage to him? The irony of his heart finally opening up, only to find there was nothing to fill the gap, was brutal.

There was no point in staying on the island, so she made plans to leave. Marrying Alejandro would make them both unhappy, if he couldn't fully unlock the feelings inside him. Goodness knew, she'd found it hard enough, but had concluded that life without love was empty. Better to risk everything than remain alone. That was her mantra, anyway. And how could warring parents raise a happy child? Better to leave now, before it came to that.

Maria was concerned about her. 'Has something happened?' she asked with a frown.

'Nothing serious,' Sienna said lightly. 'Something's come up that means I have to go back to London right away.'

Maria didn't look convinced. 'Are you sure it's nothing serious?'

'Don't worry. I'd tell you if it was.' She hated lying to Maria, but time was short, and Alejandro could walk into the kitchen at any moment. 'Travel arrangements—timing,' she murmured tensely, glancing at the clock.

'If you hurry, you might catch the last ferry,' Maria said hesitantly, as if she didn't want Sienna to leave. 'Are you sure there's nothing I can do to help?'

'Nothing, honestly.'

Seeing her resolve, Maria suggested, 'A suitcase, maybe?'

Having arrived without anything, she thought that sounded like a very good idea. 'That would be wonderful. Thank you, Maria.'

Maria missed nothing, and had probably already guessed the reason for Sienna leaving. Like everyone else, Maria must have been shocked by Alejandro's proposal. As if to confirm this, she reached out, and they hugged each other tight.

'Please don't say anything to Alejandro until the morning,' Sienna begged when they pulled apart. 'I don't want anything to spoil Tom's party. You've both gone to so much trouble to make it a success. I'll never be able to thank you enough. Tom would have loved this,' she added wistfully, glancing out of the window where the party was still in full swing.

'Tom does love it. I'm sure of that,' Maria declared with touching certainty.

A moment passed where Sienna guessed they were both thinking back to happier times with Tom, but she had to be quick if she was going to catch that ferry.

'If Alejandro asks where I am, could you say you don't know, or that you think I've gone to bed? Or, maybe say nothing at all,' she amended when Maria gave her a look.

'I'll get that suitcase for you,' Maria said, keeping whatever she thought to herself.

'Just a small one—'

Maria wheeled around, and, with a look of pure distress, pulled Sienna back into a hug. 'Just stay safe. And please stay in touch. I'll be worried about you.'

There were tears in Maria's eyes when they parted, and Sienna knew for sure that what

Maria offered was friendship in its truest form, which meant unquestioning support.

'A bird thrives best when it flies free,' Maria said.

If only Alejandro could see that too, Sienna thought as they shared one last, tight embrace.

Packing a few essentials into the suitcase Maria had delivered to her room, Sienna stowed her passport and wallet in the pocket of a riding jacket she'd borrowed from the tack room. Leaving the house, she joined a group of guests heading back to the small port town. It was a short trip from the harbour to the mainland, and from there to the airport and home.

Had she just made the biggest mistake of her life? Sienna wondered as the ferry pulled away from the dock. Refusing Alejandro's proposal was the last thing she'd do if he had shown the slightest intention of marrying for love. Tears stung her eyes as the ferry began to sway as it hit the open sea. Seeking shelter inside, she chose a row of seats at random, and sat down. It would have been better, neater for all concerned, if she had agreed to marry Alejandro.

Neater? Better? Better than what? Better than loving parents who adored their child and made it feel safe? Wasn't that worth all the money in the world, and a great deal more than a piece of paper?

She continued to argue with herself throughout the journey. Marriage to Alejandro made sense. Leaving for the unknown made no sense at all, and as a general rule Sienna was a great fan of common sense. A secure future for her baby wasn't something to dismiss lightly, but she had always been able to support herself, and why should that change now? Exchanging that sort of freedom for a life of always having to ask permission held no appeal at all, but she would have to reach an accommodation with Alejandro eventually. It would probably mean meeting face to face.

This wasn't running away, Sienna told herself firmly as the ferry picked up speed. She was running towards a new life. How could she settle for anything less than a love so powerful nothing could make it fail? A cold-blooded contract with Alejandro came nowhere near that goal. What he was proposing was worse than no love at all.

CHAPTER SIXTEEN

HAD HE ASKED too much of Sienna? A growing feeling that he had propelled him to the kitchen, where he thought she might be with Maria. He'd said goodnight to the last of their guests and wanted to share with Sienna the kind things so many had said about Tom.

That wasn't all, of course. He had to set things straight. She'd flayed the mask from his eyes, forcing him to admit, if only to himself, that he did want love, and he did want to be loved. He wanted to trust and to be trusted. He wanted children and a family, together with the chance to instil the same values in his children that his parents had instilled in him. But would any declaration of love sound false now? Sienna might think his only aim was to claim their child, and have the entire island back under his control. If he wanted her, he'd have to find a way to convince her that his feelings were genuine.

Shock slammed into him when Maria told him she'd gone.

'Gone? What do you mean, she's gone?'

'Señorita Sienna has been forced to return to England,' Maria informed him in a tone he'd never heard his loyal housekeeper use before. It was as if Maria was struggling to deliver each word with no emotion at all.

'She didn't tell you why?' he pressed with growing desperation.

'There wasn't time,' Maria intoned in the same dull voice. 'She was in a rush to catch the last ferry.'

He exhaled with disbelief. 'And didn't think to tell me this herself?'

'She didn't want to spoil the party.'

'Ha!' Shaking his head, he grimaced. Sienna had spoiled the party. He'd searched for her with growing concern until, finally, he'd convinced himself that she'd taken herself off, to be alone, or to discuss his proposal with Maria, to whom she had become increasingly close. He understood that need for space to think things through.

But not this much space.

Reining in his frustration, he held back on exposing his feelings to Maria. How would that be fair? Torment must have shown in his eyes, because Maria put a comforting hand on his arm, which was something she'd never done before.

'I thought, if she wasn't with you, she'd have gone to bed,' he admitted.

'Sienna would never leave here, until she was certain Tom's celebration was a success. She made a point of coming to thank me, and she thanked you too. I feel sure she'll be back.'

'I wish I had your certainty,' he confessed.

'If Sienna means so much to you, why are you still standing here, Alejandro? This isn't like you.'

He was thinking. Piloting his private jet would allow him to touch down in London, maybe even before Sienna, and where else would she go? 'You're right, Maria. I'll leave right away.'

Going to his study, he went through the mechanics of filing a flight plan, but by the time he replaced the receiver, he'd changed his mind. He needed to prove to Sienna that this wasn't about control, or that he was fulfilling a duty, but that she was an exceptional woman, who meant the world to him.

With a growl of frustration, he cancelled his plans. Micromanaging Sienna would never work. It might be effective in business, but exerting control over every element of such a deeply personal situation was hardly likely to convince Sienna that he was a changed man. If Sienna returned to the island, as Maria had hinted she might, it had to be because Sienna wanted to come back, and not because he could find a million different ways to persuade her.

'Yes?' he snapped, thrown by the sound of a soft tap on the door.

'I've heard from Sienna,' Maria said as she entered the room. 'She's safely back in London.'

He threw himself back in his chair with relief. There was a momentary sting in Maria's words, at the thought that Sienna had confided in Maria before him, but the most important thing was that Sienna was safe. 'Can you tell me what she said?'

As a general rule, he only had to ask and Maria would tell him anything he wanted to know, but this time she held back, and in all conscience he couldn't ask her for more. An ironic smile tipped the edges of his lips. Was it possible he was changing already?

'She sounded so excited, Alejandro, and asked us not to worry.'

'Not to worry?' Was that a joke? How was he supposed not to worry, when he cared so much?

Going to his study, he placed a call to the Blue Angel club. The manager was only too eager to tell him that he'd heard from Sienna, and they'd made plans to hold a testimonial for

Tom. Sienna would be the headline act. Desperate for her to run free, and yet in safety, Alejandro thought of other men staring at Sienna as she worked her musical magic on an audience and it hit him like a punch in the gut.

His flight to London was back on.

It was nearly time to go on stage. Mapping her still-flat stomach as she stared into the fly-blown mirror, she could only hope that, after all Maria's good food, she could still fit into one of her gowns. She wanted to look and sing her best tonight, to raise as much money as possible for the newly established Tom Slater Fund. A knock on the door of her cupboard-sized room heralded the worst possible news.

'Jason's sick?' Sienna's stomach lurched. 'Can we get another pianist in time?'

'You'll be fine. You're a professional.' The club manager told her this with the confidence of someone who had never been on stage. 'You've got backing tapes, haven't you? I've heard you use them in rehearsal.'

'In rehearsal, yes.' But tonight's performance was vital for Tom's fund.

When the going got tough… If she had to sing unaccompanied, she'd do it. She had to make this work. It was vital that tonight was a success.

She was blinded momentarily by the footlights when she walked on stage, but the wave of warm affection that greeted her reinforced her determination not to let the audience down.

She had arranged for her backing tapes to be played over the club's loudspeakers, and, even without Jason at the piano to build her confidence, she'd be fine.

Taking centre stage, she wrapped her hand around the microphone, or her comfort wand, as she often thought of it. 'Thank you all for coming tonight, and for supporting the Tom Slater Fund—' She couldn't help searching the crowd for that one special face, but, of course, Alejandro wasn't there. He was back on the island, and almost certainly furious with her for walking out.

'You don't know what this means to me,' she said. And only then noticed one particular photograph of Tom, amongst the many that the club had thoughtfully arranged on a large display. This one showed Tom and his comrades in the army. She hadn't supplied it, so who had? The last time she'd seen that photograph, it had been on Alejandro's desk.

There was no time to think about it now. Her piano introduction had started. Gathering herself, she closed her eyes, and felt the music wash over her, restoring her confidence as it flowed effortlessly from the pianist's fingertips.

The club's sound system sounded even better tonight. It was almost as if Jason were seated at the piano. And yet there were subtle differences that only a musician would register. And then a spotlight hit the piano.

'Alejandro?'

He turned briefly to face her, and dipped his chin to indicate that the introduction was over, and it was time for her to sing. By some miraculous alchemy, the power of music took her over, and, inhaling steadily, she began to sing.

The piano keys felt like old friends beneath his fingers. Jason had worked from chords, augmented by his own improvised melody, as and when required. That suited Alejandro's style of playing, and Sienna was easy to accompany. Her voice was honey sweet, with more than a hint of sultry about it, and it came as no surprise to him that when the first song had ended the audience went wild.

She glanced at him as she mentioned the name of her second song. He already had a playlist up on the piano, so he began. They were in complete union as the song progressed, until it was almost as if they were alone in the club. If only everything could be that simple, he reflected wryly as they ended the final piece in perfect harmony.

Sienna was clearly thrown when her set ended and they were finally brought face to face. She didn't know how he would react, or how he felt about the way she'd left the island. 'You were amazing,' he said to reassure her.

'You were amazing too,' she insisted. 'I've never heard you play the piano. I didn't realise you were so good. You could have been a professional musician...'

'Never mind that. I've got an idea.'

'Tell me...'

Her eyes worked their magic on his cold, unfeeling heart. Cold and unfeeling before Sienna, he amended as she continued to plumb deep. 'Why don't you do a few encores, with donations for each song?'

Her reply was to grab his hand and lead him back onto the stage.

'I think you all recognise my pianist tonight.' She had to pause for prolonged applause, while he took the chance to settle himself back at the piano. 'Alejandro has suggested that I ask you for requests, with a donation for the fund with each song. Would you do that?'

A great roar of approval greeted her suggestion.

'All in a good cause,' he added into the mic.

'The very best,' Sienna agreed, shooting him a grateful glance.

It was after midnight when they finally left the stage, but the amount of money raised was impressive, and he doubled it. 'Please,' he said, when Sienna begged him not to. 'I don't even know how you're going to pay for all this. My contribution is small by comparison with what you're going to need.'

'I'll find a way,' she said determinedly, and when her gaze switched to him, her expression softened. 'Seriously, Alejandro, thank you for tonight. I can't believe you saved the day— night—and I'm sorry I had to leave the way I did.'

'You don't have to explain,' he insisted.

'I think I do,' she argued.

'As for the playing, I enjoyed myself. It isn't every day I get the chance to play the piano at such a prestigious club.'

She smiled at that. 'Well, thank you, anyway.'

'Your thanks is all that's required.'

'Is it? Alejandro, I—'

'Don't,' he cut in. 'I won't ask you again,' he promised.

Sienna appeared suddenly diminished. They were their own worst enemies, he realised. Sienna could fill any space with the force of her will alone, but when it came to personal feelings, she was vulnerable. And what he'd proposed was a marriage of convenience. She would never accept that.

'I should go and get changed,' she said with a rueful smile as she turned in the direction of what he couldn't help but think of as her dungeon at the club. Was this how it was going to be between them now? Two sides of an island without a bridge?

'I'll wait for you,' he said.

Awareness fizzed up and down her body, making it hard to breathe. Alejandro had come to the club—to London—he'd accompanied her at the piano. It was almost too much to take in. But why was he here? Because she'd refused his proposal, or because he wanted to hear her sing, and, like her, wanted to support Tom in any way he could?

She was excited and confused as she took off her make-up. Pleased to see him didn't even begin to cover it. Being close to Alejandro again was enough—maybe had to be enough. If only they could break down all the barriers between them, to see what happened then—

'Are you ready?'

She froze, tissue suspended between her fingertips as Alejandro called to her from the other side of the door. 'Soon,' she promised, sitting back. She had to calm down before she saw him again. Calm down? Was that even possible?

Giving her hair the most perfunctory attention, she hurried to dress in her everyday clothes, relieved that she'd made a special effort tonight, for Tom's sake.

'Quite a transformation,' Alejandro observed, when she finally made it out of the boiler room. Simple trousers and a woolly sweater, to combat the London cold, together with a warm jacket she'd treated herself to a few years ago, which completed the sensible, if smart, look.

His interest scorched its way through her body. 'My car's at the front,' he informed her.

'So is my cab,' she reminded him. 'I usually time it just right, so I emerge from the club as it pulls up at the kerb. I jump in. It drives away—'

'Sounds eminently sensible to me. Why don't you take the cab, and we meet up tomorrow?'

Now she was disappointed, and her mouth dried as she suggested, 'Café next door?' Well, she'd asked for this, hadn't she? He'd proposed. She'd walked out.

'Eleven o'clock tomorrow?'

If she wanted to see him again, she had no option, but to smile and say, 'Suits me. Good-night, Alejandro…' She watched him walk away, knowing that if they could only keep a friendship between them, that would have to be enough.

Sienna's hand strayed to her stomach, where a tiny life depended on both of them to do the right thing. They would have to keep in touch, because of their baby. 'Thank you again for tonight.'

Alejandro turned around and stared at her for a long moment. And then he smiled. 'Thank *you*, Sienna. See you tomorrow at eleven.'

And then he was gone.

CHAPTER SEVENTEEN

HE GLANCED AT the clock. Four a.m.? Another seven hours before he set eyes on Sienna?

Unacceptable.

Swinging out of bed, he tugged on his jeans. Palming his keys, he quit his elegant Georgian town house to drive to an area of North London where Sienna rented a room in someone's house. Wanting to be with her clawed at his soul. Was she awake, thinking of him? Would she be alarmed when he turned up unannounced? Too bad. This was one occasion when being close to Sienna took precedence over everything. How the occupants of the house where she lived would feel when an unshaven brute banged on their door in the middle of the night remained to be seen—

Okay. Calm down. Cool off.

The streets were empty. The drive there was smooth and fast. Placing a call to Sienna, he waited. She answered on the second ring.

'Hello…?' Her voice sounded croaky and sleep-fogged.

'Did I wake you?'

He barely had chance to ask the question before Sienna exclaimed with real alarm, 'Alejandro? Are you okay? Is something wrong?'

'You could say that,' he admitted.

'Are you still there?' she pressed. Anxiety raised the pitch of her voice.

'I soon will be,' he confirmed.

'What do you mean?' She sounded confused.

'I'm driving down your street as we speak.'

'What—?'

'Put your clothes on. Let's talk. I can't wait for coffee in the morning. Okay with you?'

He sounded impatient, which was the last thing he'd intended. No control. Everything to unfold naturally. These were the rules he had given himself. If he went back to being the man who refused to wait for anything, and who never relaxed the reins of his life, he'd stand no chance with Sienna. 'Sorry, I don't mean to rush you,' he added with a frown.

She laughed, and it was such a welcome sound. 'You're sorry?' she repeated. He could hear her smiling. 'Give me five,' she added before the line cut.

Alejandro was actually outside her door. He didn't get the chance to get out of the car before she slid in beside him. 'Hi, stranger,' she teased as she climbed in.

'I missed you,' he admitted.

'You couldn't sleep?' she suggested. 'Neither could I.' She laughed, she couldn't stop the happiness bubbling out of her—or the disbelief. 'How long has it been? Five hours?'

'A lifetime,' he growled.

Firing up the engine, Alejandro checked his blind spot, and prepared to pull away. But then he stopped and shrugged as he looked at her. 'We have to come clean with each other at some point.'

However hard he tried to be serious, Alejandro's expression suggested that the next stop he'd like to make would be his bed. 'Is that what you really want? To talk?'

His lips pressed down. 'Eventually, yes.'

'Well, at least you're honest.' Was it possible to contain so much happiness? Just seeing him again, would have been enough—No, it wouldn't.

Her attention was drawn to his mouth. Alejandro was smiling.

'Just call me spontaneous.'

'Don't you mean impatient?' she suggested dryly.

He gunned the engine. 'Do you care which it is?'

'Not really. Not at all,' she confessed as

he pulled away from the kerb. Pressing back against her seat, she did ask the obvious question. 'Where are you taking me?'

'To my place?

'Sounds good to me.'

But before they had sex again, which would be the easiest thing in the world with Alejandro, she had to *know* that his sleepless night and rush to her home had less to do with sex, and *everything* to do with the fact that he had to be with her, for no other reason than he must—not that she was a responsibility, or a duty, or even that he couldn't resist taking her to bed; not even that she was the mother of his child. He must want her for herself. She wanted to be the missing part of him, as Alejandro was for her.

The elegant London square where Alejandro's imposing Georgian home was located wrapped around a small, gated park exclusive to residents. Old-fashioned gas lamps had been converted to new-fangled electricity in the latter part of the nineteenth century, adding to ambience of style and old money. It was still eerily quiet this early in the morning, and the house, when they entered, felt deserted.

'Everyone's day off,' Alejandro explained when she asked him if they were alone.

'I'd like to talk,' she said.

He shrugged. 'Whatever pleases you, Sienna.'

You please me, she thought. *That's half the problem. I've been so distracted in the past by your heart-shatteringly fabulous good looks, your air of confidence and experience, that I've barely paused to think before leaping into bed with you. But this time it's going to be different, because this time our future, and that of our child, depends on what I do next...*

It would have been the easiest thing in the world to head upstairs to Alejandro's bedroom, but when he admitted with a rueful smile, 'Trouble is, I can't think straight when you're around,' she had to laugh, because she felt the same.

'That makes two of us.'

It was only when they were inside his study that she realised how tired he looked. There was more than one night's missing sleep in Alejandro's dark, heavily fringed eyes. 'Have you slept at all recently?'

'Thanks to you?' He smiled a crooked smile. 'Not much. You?'

'Same,' she admitted.

'Because?'

'No, you go first,' she insisted.

'Because I've been a selfish—'

'Don't need to say that word.' She put a finger over his lips. 'And don't beat yourself up.

I'm just as guilty as you are, of allowing the past to rule me.'

'Survivor's guilt's no fun, is it?'

'No,' she agreed. 'But we can do something about it, you and me. Maybe not together, as I'd hoped, but—'

'What do you mean, not together?' he interrupted.

'My facility in Tom's name will be here in London, while yours will be on the island.'

'I have a better idea—'

'Trust you,' she said with a small smile.

'It was *your* idea really. *Our* facility on the island. The Tom Slater rehabilitation centre can only benefit if we combine our ideas. Your energy and mine will allow us to achieve so much more.'

She paused and frowned. 'Does that mean you accept my intention to become a working mother?'

'My mother worked, breaking horses, raising rare breeds. She worked on the ranch all her life. I don't remember anything stopping her. If I'm guilty—and I know I am—it's because I saw my mother working so hard, and I wanted something easier for my own wife.'

'Your wife?' she queried.

'Okay, I made a hash of this last time, but I never promised not to try again. And yes, Tom asked me to always look after you, but the way I feel about you has nothing to do with Tom. This is all me. And all you, I hope. I love you, Sienna, and my sense of duty has nothing to do with that. I love you as I have never loved in all my life. I hope you can believe me now?'

She did believe him, and a great well of happiness opened inside her when Alejandro drew her close for a tender kiss. This was swiftly followed by concern for him. Was she really responsible for those deep black circles beneath his eyes?

'I know you said we'd go to bed after we talked, but, honestly, Alejandro, I really think you need to sleep.'

'I will,' he promised with a look that melted her from the inside out.

'I do have one stipulation,' he said.

'Which is?' she queried.

'We sleep in the same bed.'

'Are you short of bedrooms here?' she teased.

He shrugged. 'I'm short of affection.'

Her heart went out to him. 'There's only one thing we can do about this…'

'Which is?'

'We sleep together,' she said.

Sleeping together wouldn't be easy, but did she want to change things up, or not? There had to be more than sex between them.

'Is sleep enough for you?' he asked with a wicked glint in his tired eyes.

She told him straight. 'Your love is enough for me.'

She'd borrowed one of Alejandro's tee shirts, which was around ten sizes too large. And kept her underwear on. Alejandro had no such reservations and stripped off completely. As torture went, that was extreme. And did he have to lie there like Adonis, with his hands tucked behind his head, displaying his ridiculously impressive torso, as if this were just another night for him?

'You don't have to hang onto the edge of the bed,' he advised. 'I don't bite—unless you want me to?'

'That won't be necessary, thank you,' she replied primly, not daring to move an inch.

'Come over here,' he said in a very different tone. 'Don't you know by now that you can trust me?'

She did.

Feeling Alejandro, warm and strong, pressed up against her, was the most extreme and wonderful feeling in the world. Everything they had between them was based on trust. And wasn't that the crux of it all?

He didn't sleep for what remained of that night. He preferred to watch Sienna sleep. Breathing steadily, with all her muscles relaxed. It was a privilege to guard her and their child.

Before the early morning light could wake her, he carefully disentangled himself and left the bed. His alarming erection would just have to alarm itself. He took a shower, eyes closed, face turned up to the icy spray.

And then she joined him.

'Could you turn the heat up?' she asked.

He certainly could.

'You can't hide how you feel about me,' she said.

'Full disclosure?' he agreed as he swept an arm around her waist. Cupping the back of her head, he brought her close. He did wonder for a moment if he was rushing things, when Sienna put her hands palms flat against his chest, but it was the weakest push ever, and her fingers soon closed around his.

Dipping her head, she nipped each of his nipples in turn, before telling him, 'Why should you have all the fun?'

Why, indeed?

Standing on tiptoe, she brushed a kiss against his lips. Being bathed in steam added an edge to sensation. Parting her lips with his tongue, he kissed her. She swayed against him. Closing his teeth lightly over Sienna's kiss-swollen bottom lip, he made her whimper. She clung to him tightly, until, nudging his erection with the lightest brushes of her body, she finally thrust her hips towards him.

If Alejandro continued to stroke the curve of her buttocks as he was doing right now, she refused to be accountable for her actions. Every erotic zone she possessed was screaming for attention. Arching her back, she offered herself shamelessly, only to pull away the moment Alejandro wanted to take her, knowing that when she rubbed her breasts against his muscular chest, it was torture for both of them.

'I want you,' she said, reaching up. Weaving her fingers through his thick black hair, she kept him close. 'Kiss me, and don't pull away this time,' she warned.

'Who's pulling away?' Alejandro gave a deep, sexy laugh. 'Who's teasing me, and torturing themselves into the bargain?'

'If you dare make me wait—' She gasped with relief as Alejandro took over.

Dismissing the last rational thought from her head, he rasped his early-morning stubble against her neck, increasing her arousal. She wanted to feel that friction against every part of her—Well, maybe not *every* part of her, but she'd tell him when and where to stop.

Turned out, she didn't need to give Alejandro any advice, as his touch, as always, was both exquisite and exquisitely intuitive. Running a thumb pad over her bottom lip, he traced the line of her mouth where his stubble had abraded her. 'Did I hurt you with my kisses?'

'No,' was all she could manage to gasp before drawing him back for more kisses.

Warm water continued to tumble down, enveloping them, caressing them, adding to their mutual arousal. Alejandro's eyelashes were clotted together, while his mouth and strong white teeth, and that wicked smile, became yet another aphrodisiac, and one she hardly needed. Closing her eyes, she suggested, 'Why don't you kiss it better?'

'Your poor sore mouth, or somewhere else?'

'Make a start and I'll let you know.'

His smile was long and lazy. 'I'm going to start by soaping you down, and then we'll see what happens...'

'Start anywhere you like. Just don't keep me waiting.'

Some gorgeous-smelling shower gel later— 'Vanilla and rosemary,' Alejandro revealed— and she was suspended on a plateau of erotic pleasure.

'I think you like this,' he said.

'I like everything you do to me, she admitted.

Soaping the length of her spine made her arch her back in an attempt to draw Alejandro's attention to the one place that needed him most. And at last, *at last*, he responded as she'd desperately hoped he would.

'Better?' he asked straight-faced.

'Not nearly,' she warned. Was she going to waste that formidable erection? Even with Sienna's determination, she had to bury her face against Alejandro's chest to remind herself that she could take him and that she'd done so before. But he continued to soap her, denying her the satisfaction she craved. Admittedly, being brushed intimately with a sponge controlled by Alejandro was quite a sensory experience, but she'd had enough of teasing and took him in hand.

Lifting her, Alejandro pressed her against the cool wall tiles. Wrapping her legs around his waist, she groaned in ecstasy as he took her with infinite care. He knew just how to move slowly, rotating his hips until she couldn't hold on.

'Okay?' he asked, plunging deeper still. 'And now?'

A wail of intense pleasure pealed from her throat as he massaged her beyond the point of control. When she lost it, he captured her wrists in one big fist, pinning them against the wall, while he supported and directed her buttocks with his other hand.

'Yes! *Yes!*' Oblivion. Blissful oblivion, filled with pleasure that went on and on.

'Better now,' he said with confidence.

She smiled up into his laughing eyes. 'What do you think, Alejandro?'

'I think I want to kiss you.' Tipping her chin up, he kissed her with surprising gentleness. She sensed a real change in him. It was as if Alejandro knew all her fears, and how to banish them. 'Do you trust me totally now?' he whispered against her mouth.

'You know I do.'

It seemed incredible that they were being so intimate in the shower, sharing their innermost feelings while warm water pounded down. She could marry this man, Sienna realised, but he would have to do a lot better with his proposal.

'Why are you laughing?' he asked.

'I'm laughing with happiness, because of who we are, and how we've stupidly allowed the past to influence our actions and thinking for so long. We're as bad as one another, allowing suspicion and lack of trust to rule us. Fear of loving too much, in case that love is cruelly ripped away, is just another way of punishing ourselves. And it's time to stop,' she said with feeling, staring directly into his eyes.

Switching off the shower, Alejandro reached for a towel, and swaddled her. 'Is this leading up to you proposing to me?' he suggested. 'Or are you giving me a second chance?'

'If I do, it has to be because you don't want to share your life with anyone else. It can't have anything to do with your loyalty to Tom, or the fact that I'm expecting your child. It has to be as necessary as breathing, and as right in your eyes as the sun rising on each new day.'

'Someone should have warned me that you're a romantic,' he teased, pulling her in front of him to drop a kiss on her lips. 'But I'm sorry for being clumsy. Out of practice on the proposal front, I guess.'

'You make a habit of proposing to random women?' They were both smiling, and something told Sienna that this time Alejandro would get it absolutely right.

'I'm better at giving instructions than expressing myself—'

'No way,' she said, pretending surprise.

'That doesn't mean I can't change,' Alejandro insisted, turning serious now. 'And, if I've got it hopelessly wrong in the past, I hope you believe me now, when I tell you how much I love you—that I can't live without you—and if you'll marry me, you'll make me the happiest man on earth.'

'Because?' she probed, quivering on the edge of happiness.

'Because your love has saved me,' Alejandro explained with an honest shrug. 'You, Sienna Slater, have managed the impossible. You've saved me from myself.'

'Well, now we're into true confessions, you helped me find myself again. I'm no one's little sister, but I could be someone's wife.'

'My wife,' Alejandro husked against her mouth.

'You don't find me too challenging?'

'Of course, but that's the wake-up call I need. I realise now that I've been waiting for you, and that a perfectly imperfect woman suits perfectly imperfect me. Besides,' he said as he drew her back into his arms, 'I'm sure I can tame you out of all those challenges in time.'

'Lucky for you, I'm happy to let you believe that,' Sienna teased back.

'Seriously, Sienna. You lifted me when I was down. You raised me up, forcing me to confront emotion head-on. Without it, what would we be? Cardboard cut-outs? Cartoons? Emotion is a gift I'm happy to embrace. Where you're concerned, I can't imagine life without it. I love you, Sienna, with all my heart, and I can't imagine life without you. Admittedly, that wasn't how I felt to begin with.'

'Nor me,' Sienna agreed with a wry smile.

'But it's how you make me feel now that matters,' Alejandro insisted with a long, steady look into her eyes. 'Let's always look forward. You're irreplaceable and unique, and if you won't agree to live with me, I'll have no option but to live with you.'

'In my bedsit in North London?'

'Willingly,' Alejandro exclaimed.

'Now I do know you're joking.'

'I'm being absolutely serious. I'd do anything for you. Not just because I want children, or want to have those children with you. And this has nothing to do with our joint ambition to build something in Tom's name that will benefit countless people who suffered as he did. This is purely about you and me.'

'And our joint ambition,' she said with love.

Securing a towel around his waist, Alejandro laughed. 'You don't think I'd allow you to embark on some crazy project without me, do you?'

She swiped at him with a towel. 'You'd better be joking.'

Binding her arms with his, Alejandro kissed her and teased her until she was crying with laughter. 'Combining our talents will make everything so much better, and we'll reach our goal faster in the end.'

'I'm not sure what your goal is right now,' she admitted, feeling Alejandro growing hard again.

'We'll discuss that too,' he promised.

There was something different in Alejandro's eyes, a gentle truth she'd never seen before. 'A joint project?' she confirmed.

'Two joint projects,' he said, reminding her with many kisses about their baby. 'And a wedding to arrange—if the only woman I could ever love will have me?'

Was it possible for a heart to explode with love?

'Well, what do you think?' Alejandro pressed.

'I think we take it one thing at a time.'

CHAPTER EIGHTEEN

'OKAY, SO THIS is a proposal in three parts,' Alejandro informed her. 'Part one—'

'Alejandro, what are you doing?'

Freshly showered, jeans, shirt with the sleeves rolled up, barefoot, *and* on his knees? While she was still snuggled up in bed.

'Will you marry me?' he said, all humour stripped from his face. Replacing the humour was a steady beam of love.

'Will I—? Seriously, Alejandro—'

'Seriously. I don't have a ring yet, so will this do?'

The flowers his London housekeeper loved to leave around the house had been called into use, Sienna noticed. Having woven one of the vines into a ring—with not such surprising dexterity—Alejandro slipped the green circle onto Sienna's wedding finger.

'I haven't said yes yet,' she pointed out. But

snatching his hand back, she kissed his palm. 'But I love you.'

'You will say yes,' he told her confidently. 'You'll say yes here in London, where it's my aim to dispel every shadow you first found in this house. And you'll say yes in Spain, when you're in my bed—'

'I'll say yes more than once when I'm in your bed,' she observed with a happy frown. 'You're serious about this, aren't you?'

'Never more so,' Alejandro assured her as he joined her on the bed. 'Anyway, get up now, and don't bother packing. We'll pick up what you need when we're there.'

'Where?'

'Oh, I don't know—Rome, Paris, Milan, Monte Carlo—wherever the whim takes us.'

'Alejandro,' she mock scolded, shaking her head. 'Tell me where we're going, so I know what clothes to wear.'

'Come as you are.'

'Naked?'

'There aren't too many paparazzi outside—'

'You're impossible,' she protested with a happy growl.

'Yes, I am, and so are you, which is why we get on so well.'

'Do we?'

'You know we do.' Cupping her face in his

hands, he kissed her with lingering devotion. 'Be quick,' he whispered against her mouth when he released her.

Alejandro's butler opened the door to his home in Mayfair when they returned after a short, passionate break. All the curtains were open, and light was flooding in as they crossed the hall.

'Is everything ready?' Alejandro asked his assembled staff.

'Ready,' they choroused, welcoming Sienna with the warmest of smiles.

'What's ready?' she asked, excitement rising as Alejandro led her into his library.

She gasped. 'I've never seen so many flowers in my life.' The entire room was full of the most glorious floral displays, the scent and sight of which completely dazzled her.

'Have you ever seen so many diamonds before?' Alejandro enquired, as if he were asking her about snowflakes on a lawn. He was standing at his library table where the most fabulous selection of diamond rings was displayed. 'Choose,' he insisted. 'Have them all, if you want.'

If she'd been dazzled by flowers, she needed eye protection to study the gems on display. 'But I'm happy with this one,' she said, staring at the vine band on her finger. She was marrying Alejandro for love, not for diamonds.

'But it wouldn't hurt to wear my ring for the rest of your life, would it? So, choose one...' Taking hold of her hand, he knelt on one knee. She dropped to her knees in front of him.

'Yes,' she whispered, staring into the eyes of the man she loved with all her heart. 'Yes, I will marry you, but not because of diamond rings. I choose you. I choose this.' Raising her hand with its band of green vine still intact, she explained with a shrug. 'I don't need anything else. I never have. I only need you.'

Alejandro groaned as he stood up. 'Don't tell me, you're going to take as long to accept my ring as you've taken to accept me?'

'I won't have to train a ring,' she pointed out, tongue in cheek.

'Have you trained me sufficiently now?'

She frowned. 'I think it might be a lifetime commitment.'

'I can be very persuasive,' he said, taking her back to the rings.

'And I can be stubborn,' she admitted, 'but not when it comes to telling the man I love that I appreciate everything he does for me.'

Alejandro swung her into his arms, making sure that their lips met in the first kiss of a whole new story.

It would have been the wedding of the century, if she'd allowed Alejandro to have his way. They didn't need to show the world how much they loved each other, when that was self-evident. To Sienna's surprise, Maria disagreed. They were back at the ranch house in Spain, where the wedding was due to take place the following month.

'What would your mother want for you?' Maria asked in her usual forthright manner.

'A fairy-tale wedding,' Sienna admitted. They'd always talked about it when they played dress-up. Her mother would take the part of queen, while Sienna played the role of feisty princess in need of a suitable prince. They'd ride off on their snowy white ponies, to find a man 'to bring home the bacon', as her mother so colourfully put it—Or a suitable vegan substitute, Sienna thought now with a happy laugh. Either way, women always took the lead role in their fantasies.

'Then a fairy-tale wedding is what you shall have,' Maria decreed. 'You and Alejandro have hidden your feelings away long enough. It's time to show the world how you feel about each other. It's time to inspire and lead,' Maria finished with a decisive gesture.

Sienna was outnumbered when Alejandro agreed. 'Don't I have any say in this?' she pleaded.

'Yes, you can decide whether to travel to

Rome, Paris, or Milan to choose your gown,' Alejandro conceded. 'If you don't like anything there, you can return to London, to visit the couturier favoured by the royal family.'

'Oh, can I?' Sienna said, rallying fast. 'How about this—Maria, will you make my gown?'

'Well, I—'

Maria glanced anxiously at Alejandro, who gave an accepting shrug. 'Maria?' he pressed. 'Would you do that for us?'

'With the greatest of pleasure,' Maria enthused as she enveloped Sienna in a bear hug. 'It will be both my pride and my pleasure.'

Sienna's wedding gown *was* the most beautiful gown she'd ever seen. A simple sheath of ivory silk, it skimmed her body like a dream, whispering over her skin like the lightest touch of Alejandro's fingers. With her hair flowing free, and a coronet of fresh flowers, she carried a bouquet of glorious white peonies.

The wedding was held in a marquee on Alejandro's estancia on the island, on the banks of the sparkling river, where very soon the Tom Slater Concert Hall would be built. A floral arch marked the exact spot where the stage would be located, and Jason supplied the music on Clara Schumann's Biedermeier piano as Sienna walked down the petal-strewn aisle—on no one's arm, because there was only one man, one heart, one love she would allow to lead her anywhere, and then, only when they agreed he could, she reflected wryly with a heart full of love as Alejandro reached out to take her hand in his.

But they did have one addition to Alejandro's security team. Rex from the club, and if he and Maria were occasionally seen out together, strolling along the banks of the beautiful river, well, that was fate, Sienna concluded, and fate could be kinder than you expected sometimes.

Alejandro's eyes filled with tears at the sight of his beautiful wife. He wasn't ashamed of that emotion, and could only thank the fates for bringing them together.

'Our future will be, oh, so worthwhile,' Sienna whispered when he placed the simple diamond band she'd chosen on her wedding finger.

This was what it meant to have a family, he reflected after they kissed; this was what it meant to come home.

Turning to face their guests, he smiled. His brothers and sister were smiling back at him, with an expression on his brothers' faces that suggested, why did you take so long? They were right, no more waiting. Bringing Sienna into his arms, he whispered, 'Thank you for saving me.' From what might have been such an arid life, but which was now full of boundless possibility.

'I love you,' she whispered, staring her truth into his eyes.

'And I love you more than life itself,' he replied.

EPILOGUE

A little over three years later...

EVERY CHRISTMAS FROM now on should include a family gathering at the Tom Slater Concert Hall. Sienna decided this as she watched her own children, together with her nephews and nieces by marriage, having the time of their lives. There was so much space here, so much light, and Alejandro had arranged the entertainment, making sure there was something for everyone. He'd booked children's entertainers, film shows, petting zoos, spa treatments, and now they were all playing the most ridiculous charades that had everyone in hysterics, and even more ridiculous quiz games where everyone cheated, and, of course, there would be the inevitable polo match to follow.

Alejandro had insisted on including the children of everyone who worked for him, which made everything so much warmer and more special, Sienna thought. He'd even flown in families who worked in the UK—though on this occasion his butler was not wearing white gloves, and looked a different and very happy man in blue jeans.

Smiling around, she felt the warmth of the Acosta family envelop her, as it had from the start. The Acosta men's wives, and Alejandro's sister, Sofia, had accepted Sienna without question, and with great enthusiasm. 'About time!' Sofia had declared, giving her brother a hug. 'I've got you back at last. Thank you, Sienna.'

Lucia had been wonderful, on hand for advice with each new Acosta baby. They had become the closest of friends. Sienna made Alejandro happy, and that was all his family cared about. She'd even headed up a team at the last polo match that had thrashed the Acosta men— though whether the guys' team riding reversed in the saddle counted as cheating, she couldn't possibly say.

Sienna and Alejandro had been blessed with three children. Carlos, the oldest, was nearly three, while twins Ellie and Tiago, who were currently fast asleep by her side in their Moses baskets, would soon be crawling, creating happy chaos with their cousins. Laughing, she covered her ears in mock horror when the children started to scream with excitement as Alejandro made the announcement that it was time for presents.

A storm of wrapping paper later, silence fell as toys were assembled, and everyone was absorbed in investigating their gifts. Sienna had bought a new bridle for Alejandro, as well as a headband for his favourite horse.

'And I've got nothing for you,' he observed with a frown.

'Do you really think I need anything more than this?' she asked, looking around. 'And on top of this, staff for the facility is already in place and ready to start working with our first visitors, and foundations have been laid for our site in London. That's more than enough for me.'

'Lucky for you,' Alejandro observed, 'that there's more pleasure in giving than receiving.'

Sienna smiled at the man she loved. How many times had they proven that between them?

'As it happens, I have got something for you,' Alejandro revealed. Delving into the back pocket of his jeans, he brought out a small midnight-blue velvet box. 'And don't say you don't need this,' he scolded with a grin, 'because you're going to get it, whether you want it or not. We both know your vine ring disappeared on the day Carlos was born.'

'I was frightened he might chew on it.'

'He'll be quite safe chewing on this.'

As Alejandro flipped the lid of the ring case she gasped with amazement. 'Alejandro! What have you done?'

'Arranged for you to have the most beautiful diamond ring in the world. It used to belong to my mother.'

'I'll treasure it,' she vowed.

The blue-white sparkle of the pear-shaped diamond was mesmerising. It was easily the most beautiful ring Sienna had ever seen, but its sentimental value made it all the more precious.

'Do you like it, *mi querida*?' Alejandro asked as he hunkered down at her side.

'I love it,' she breathed as he slipped the magnificent jewel onto her finger. 'But that's not even close to how much I love you.'

'For ever,' Alejandro whispered as he drew her close for a kiss.

'And always,' she breathed.

* * * * *